Blackwing Beast

(Kane's Mountains, Book 3)

T. S. JOYCE

Blackwing Beast

ISBN-13: 978-1539499947
ISBN-10: 1539499944
Copyright © 2016, T. S. Joyce
First electronic publication: October 2016

T. S. Joyce
www. tsjoyce.com

All Rights Are Reserved. No part of this book may be used or reproduced in any manner whatsoever without written permission, except in the case of brief quotations embodied in critical articles and reviews. The unauthorized reproduction or distribution of this copyrighted work is illegal. No part of this book may be scanned, uploaded or distributed via the Internet or any other means, electronic or print, without the author's permission.

NOTE FROM THE AUTHOR:

This book is a work of fiction. The names, characters, places, and incidents are products of the writer's imagination or have been used fictitiously and are not to be construed as real. Any resemblance to persons, living or dead, actual events, locale or organizations is entirely coincidental. The author does not have any control over and does not assume any responsibility for third-party websites or their content.

Published in the United States of America

First digital publication: October 2016
First print publication: October 2016

Editing: Corinne DeMaagd
Cover Photography: Furious Fotog
Cover Model: Tyler Halligan

DEDICATION

For the other half of TnT.

ACKNOWLEDGMENTS

I couldn't write these books without some amazing people behind me. This book was a hard one for me. It's the end of this huge thirty-three book saga that started in Damon's Mountains, and I had trouble saying goodbye to this universe. But there were people behind the scenes who kept me on track. A huge thanks to Corinne DeMaagd, for helping me to polish my books, and for being an amazing and supportive friend. We both worked really hard on this in edits to make sure I got this right. And thanks to Furious Fotog for getting this shot for the cover. I asked him and the cover model to do this shot, and they came through in a big way for me. Speaking of the cover model...I got lucky enough to meet Tyler Halligan, and sign at events with him, and he's become a steadying force behind the scenes. Thank you Ty for keeping me sane. To my little team, my family, who put up with so much to share me with these characters, you have my heart.

And last but never least, thank you, awesome reader. You have done more for me and my stories than I can even explain on this teeny page. You found my books, and ran with them, and every share, review, and comment makes release days so incredibly special to me.

1010 is magic and so are you.

ONE

Kiera Pierce's heart was hammering so hard against her sternum, she was sure the shifters across the room would hear her.

Danny's BBQ was hopping today, which was irritating because people kept walking through her line of sight, blocking out the Blackwing Crew. She liked being able see them at all times. Survivors kept their eyes on danger.

God, it was good to see Kane again. Good and emotional. And then hard and good again, on an endless loop. She'd known him very well once in a facility called Apex Genetic Testing. They'd both lost everything there, but Kane hadn't stayed down—not like her. Kane had found his dragon again.

Kiera, on the other hand, was stuck in a spiral, like a helicopter that had been clipped in the air and was crashing to earth in an uncontrolled tailspin. She was close to impact, and desperation said that Dark Kane and his crew of monsters might be her last chance to keep her sanity.

She'd done her research before she began her steady stalk of Kane a month ago.

Registered to his crew: Winter Donovan, black panther shifter, grew up in the city so she was probably all kinds of fucked up. Killed her own dad trying to Turn him. Claimed by a panther in Red Havoc who didn't keep her, then landed in Kane's crew a few months ago with her new mate, Logan.

Logan Furrow: Grade-A psychopath. He was an arsenic-laced jagged pill. Former mercenary whose job was to put down problem shifters, so his bear was no doubt broken beyond repair. And Winter was sporting one gnarly bear claw claiming mark across her arm. Oh, she must be proud enough since she was wearing a tank top in the middle of winter, but it looked brutal. It was the worst claiming mark Kiera had ever seen, and by a lot.

Dustin Porter: Former submissive werewolf in

the Valdoro pack. The entire pack, including his brother, were burned and turned to ashes. The dick weevils probably deserved it. God, she hated werewolves. Dustin had betrayed his pack to join the Blackwings. Right now, he looked riled up, one eye glowing blue, the other green, his lip snarled as he popped off to Logan, who also looked way too bloodthirsty for her taste. The idiots were probably going to fight right here in front of all these humans. They had brawled at nearly every place she'd stalked them.

Emma Porter, new Bride of Frankenwolf, formerly human, raised in a freaking coven of vampires, Turned a few months ago when the Blackwings went to war with not one, but three packs. Hearing impaired in her human form, but that didn't seem to slow her at all. She was sitting right in the middle of the crew, holding her own, popping off, reading lips like a champ. Tiny foul-mouthed hellion and, from what Kiera could tell, a good match for her mate, who was now standing with his arms locked on the table as he yelled at Logan about how, "I'm not sharing my jalapeño sausages with you ever again!" He could've been making a dick joke, Kiera couldn't tell. He made a lot of them.

Last but not least, the dragons themselves. Kane Reeves, aka the End of Days, aka Dark Kane, aka The Darkness, aka The Motherfuckin' Apocalypse. Geez, just from that list of names, she would've tucked tail and run, except she'd known him once. He'd been soft-spoken, protective, and kind—at least when his dragon wasn't trying to burn down the facility with everyone in it, including her. He probably wouldn't even recognize her now. The years had changed her infinitely.

Rowan Barnett rounded out the crew. Second in the Blackwings, proud mate of Dark Kane, sweet, but she was no pushover. She was equally dangerous but had better control. Kiera could tell from her calm demeanor. Currently, Kane looked like he was about to throttle Logan and Dustin, who were arguing even louder. Something about the best flavor of sausage. Dustin had flipped Logan off twice, while Logan had a vein throbbing in his beet-red forehead. Yep, they were definitely going to fight. And what were the girls in the crew doing? Laughing. *Way to go Kane. Steller crew you put together.*

But wait. A tall man with massive shoulders

strode from the counter directly to the table where the Blackwings sat. She'd never seen him before in all the time she'd spent stalking Kane and his merry band of lunatics. There was no one else registered to the crew, but this one was obviously a shifter. Even with her weakened senses, she could feel how heavy his dominance was. It lifted the fine hairs on the back of her neck. She only got his profile as he pulled a chair loudly across the wood floor and spun it backward, then sat, plopping his mountain of barbecue on the table. His face was perfect—beautiful really. Flawless and symmetrical, high cheek bones, eyes large but slightly slanted. Feline perhaps. A short beard, reddish blond, covered his chiseled jaw and moved as he cursed Logan and Dustin out. "Sit down," he barked out, jamming a finger at Dustin. "This is why I never want to fuckin' hang out with you. You're all exhausting."

"But you love us," Winter said with a mushy smile.

"Why do you keep saying that?" the man asked, looking pissed.

Kiera cocked her head and studied him. If he was a Blackwing, he hadn't registered yet. And if that was the case, why not?

He was tall with powerful legs and a short, blond crop of hair on his head. Despite the early January chill, he wore no jacket, only a tight black sweater with the sleeves rolled up to his elbows. Tattoos covered his hands as he slapped a pound of brisket between two pathetically small slices of bread. He was snarling loud enough that the humans at the table behind him scooted farther down the bench seat away from him.

Surprised, Kiera huffed a soft laugh at the looks on their concerned faces. Laughing felt good. She hadn't done that in... God, when was the last time? She barely recognized the sound coming from herself. It was hard not to find the humor in this effed-up crew of monsters, though, because clearly this muscled-up, pissed-off behemoth was the cherry on top of Kane's Psychopath Sunday. This crew wouldn't make it a year without killing each other.

Dustin stabbed Logan in the hand with a fork. Obviously he had a death wish. Winter and Rowan weren't laughing anymore, but instead pushed against Logan's chest as he stood. Idiots were gonna make the news again. Kiera lifted the newspaper she'd been hiding behind up higher to cover her smile.

The sexy berserker shook his head as if he'd seen this game too many times and didn't care to play anymore. He went back to eating, even as Dustin and Logan locked up over the table. Food went flying when the whole thing scooted hard across the floor, but the pretty man only lifted his tray with a tired sigh. And then slowly, he turned his head and looked directly at Kiera.

She was horrified by what she saw. The other side of his face was ruined, scarred with deep, red claw marks that stretched from his hairline to his jaw, missing his eye by mere millimeters. But that wasn't the most terrifying thing that struck her. This was a two-parter. One, his eyes were the glowing gold of a lion shifter, and two, she recognized him. Beast—the nightmare of her people. Or who her people should've been had her own lioness not been stripped from her in Apex.

Terrified, Kiera gasped and jerked the newspaper in front of her face. He'd cut his hair. That's why she hadn't recognized him. He used to wear it longer. He used to be the poster boy for the perfect male lion shifter specimen, and then he'd gone insane. He'd gone dangerous. He'd killed his pride.

Fuck. She needed to go. She couldn't do this. Not if Beast was in this crew. Kiera was in trouble, but not that much. This was like jumping from one boiling hot pot of water into an active volcano. Nope. She stood so fast the bench seat behind her nearly toppled over. When she dropped the newspaper, Beast was there, sitting across the table from her eating as though he'd been there for an hour. "Sit," he growled.

Oh, she wanted to obey him, which pissed her off. He wasn't her alpha. She didn't even have an animal anymore, so this dominance bullshit wasn't going to work on her. "Fuck you," she spat out. Then she turned to leave. God, it was hard giving the monster her back. It went against every screaming instinct she had.

"Alana's Coffee Shop, the Outdoor Center, Drat's three times, Cork and Bean Bistro, Wanda's Waffle House, the grocery store for every beer run Kane's made in the last month, and River's Edge. Twice."

Kiera froze. He'd just listed every place she'd

watched the Blackwing Crew. Slowly, she turned and dared a look into his hollow, golden eyes.

Beast arched his blond brows and repeated sternly, "Sit."

She cast a quick, calculating glance at the Blackwings in the back corner. They weren't fighting anymore. They were staring at her. And Dark Kane wore a frown. If he didn't recognize her yet, he was going to work it out soon.

Carefully, Kiera sat, placing Beast's massive shoulders between her and the alpha of the Blackwings. She wasn't ready to deal with Kane. Maybe she never would be.

"How did you know I was following them?"

"Stalking," Beast corrected around a bite of brisket sandwich. "Call it what it is, little human with the strange-colored eyes. I like to stalk to. You've been fun."

Shit. She shouldn't have sat. Beast's mouth was sexy when he ate. *Stop it.* It was the hormones talking. He was a murderer. The air was like water, drowning her with each breath she tried to drag into her lungs.

Beast gulped the bite and leaned his elbows on

the table with a bang. His blazing eyes tightened at the corners. "Why are you watching the D-Team?"

"The D-Team?" If she hadn't been terrified, she would've laughed. *Of course,* Kane's crew was called the D-Team.

Beast cocked his head thoughtfully. "What's wrong with you? You smell sick, or...something."

"That's none of your business, and you won't have to worry about me trailing your D-Team anymore. I'm leaving tonight."

His nostrils flared slightly as he inhaled, and his frown deepened. "Probably best. The gig's up and all. The Blackwings will have your scent memorized now, so stalking won't work."

Kiera stood to leave, but he grabbed her hand suddenly. A burst of heat shocked right through his fingertips and jolted up her arm. "Why are you so scared?" he asked.

Right now? There were a dozen different reasons, but none she wanted to admit to this murderer. Kiera yanked her hand out of his grasp and rubbed the tingling skin where he'd touched her.

"Is it because of the scars?" he asked frankly, but he shook his head and answered his own question.

"No, it's not that. You've barely looked at them. You've stayed right in my eyes. You smell scared, but you hold my gaze. Human instincts warn you I'm dangerous, but then you hold my gaze. No one does that. Why you?"

"Maybe I'm a broken human."

Beast cocked his head. "Truth."

I'm scared because I know who you are. The words were right there on her tongue, but uttering them would get her killed by this man. He was hiding in Kane's Mountains for a reason, and that reason was rivers of blood on his hands. Her death would mean nothing to him. It wouldn't be a black mark on his soul because it was already dark as pitch.

"Kiera?" Kane asked loudly. He was standing now, his eyes sparking with recognition, and, oh shit, she could not do this. It was way past time to go.

She spun and strode for the door, threw it open, and sprinted for her black El Camino. She'd merely heard her name uttered from her old friend's lips, and already her heart was shredding to pieces. She should have never come to find Kane. She should've just let the past die. Kiera pressed her hand over her fluttering stomach and yanked her driver's side door open. But before she could get in, the door slammed out of her hands, and the El Camino rocked as Dustin settled into the bed. Beast stood with his giant hand splayed on the door and a snarl in his throat. Someone spun her around and pulled her into a back-breaking hug. Kane smelled just the same.

A sob worked up Kiera's throat, and she clutched onto his shirt, desperate to push him away and hold him tighter all at once.

"I tried to find you," Kane rumbled.

She was staining his shirt with her tears. "I didn't want anyone to find me after... I just needed to be alone," she whispered in broken words.

"All this time?"

Feeling weak, she shoved off him and wiped her cheeks with her sweater sleeve. Her stomach hurt so bad. A wave of nausea took her, and she retched near the left headlight of her ride. When nothing came out, she squatted down and linked her hands behind her hair.

"Are you sick?" Kane asked.

"Is it an STD?" Dustin asked.

"Leave us," Kane demanded of the Blackwings, all gathered around them now.

"I don't like this," Beast murmured low to Kane. "Something's wrong with her. I don't like you this close to her."

The murderer had protective instincts. That was a surprise. Kiera stood and smoothed her hair back away from her face. A thin sheen of cold sweat had spread across her forehead. She felt like death warmed over, but that was her new normal. "I'm no threat to your alpha."

"She's my friend," Kane murmured.

"From where?" Rowan Barnett asked from behind him. From the compassionate look in her blue eyes, she likely already knew.

Kane sighed and crossed his arms over his chest. Looking so sad, he mumbled, "Apex."

"Shhhhit," Beast murmured. He stood ramrod straight, his chest rising and falling too fast. His eyes were so bright it hurt to look at them. "You were a shifter?"

Kiera looked off into the woods near the restaurant. That was nobody's damn business, and how rude of him for asking.

"What animal?" Beast asked low.

"Beast," Rowan said softly, sliding her hand over

his bicep.

The titan shook her off and asked louder, "What animal, *Kiera*?"

Her throat was so tight it was hard to get the word out. "Lioness."

"No," Beast said, shaking his head in denial. "No! Kane I'm not doing this. She has to go."

"What?" Kane asked.

"No lions here. None but me."

"She was stripped of the animal," Rowan said, anger blasting through her voice like shrapnel.

"Doesn't matter, it's too fucking close." Beast was panicking. Even Kiera could smell it. He was backing up on the gravel lot, pace by stumbling pace. His emotion filled eyes and those pinpoint pupils were trained on her. "Please go," he choked out. His voice dipped to a ragged whisper. "Please." And then Beast turned and strode for a bright blue Ford Raptor, got in, slammed the door, and peeled out of the lot, spraying gravel as he went.

"And biggest asshole trophy still goes to Beast," Dustin said, his work boot propped on the edge of the El Camino bed as he watched the truck disappear down the road. He turned to Kiera, his long, sandy-blond hair whipping in the cold breeze. "You want some sausage?"

"Dustin, really?" Winter asked.

Dustin threw up his hands, feigning innocence. "Not a dick joke that time, I swear. I can hear her stomach growling from here." He made a circle with his fingers over his head like a halo and smiled sweetly. "Today I'm being an angel."

"You started another fight with me in Danny's," Logan growled. "Your halo is broken into horn shapes."

Dustin narrowed his eyes and flipped Logan off. Again.

"Also angels don't give the finger," Winter pointed out.

Kane looked pissed, and his eyes were now that bright dragon green with the elongated pupils. "Did no one hear my order to leave us alone?"

Emma, the hearing-impaired one, raised her hand with a crooked smile on her lips. "I did."

Kane shook his head, called them, "smart-asses," then jammed his finger back toward the restaurant. "Leave! Now!" Power crackled through his words. Even Kiera could feel the command in his tone.

Kiera was having a hard time dragging her gaze away from where Beast's truck had disappeared. "What's wrong with him?" she asked Kane as the others meandered inside.

Kane hooked his hands on his hips and followed her gaze. With a shrug, he muttered, "A lot of stuff. It's not personal, though, Kiera. He's...troubled." He twitched his chin toward his crew. "They all are."

"But not you. Not anymore."

Kane huffed a tired sound. "Or maybe I'm the worst one. Are you in some kind of danger?"

The question caught her off guard, so she hesitated before she nodded.

Kane reached forward and touched her dyed locks. She'd grown her hair out since they'd shaved it at Apex, colored her fair hair dark with a deep purple sheen all over. When he pushed up the side of her hair, she knew what he was looking for. He was searching for the scars from Apex. The ones that were part of the program to *cleanse* her, as the humans called it. The scars that helped to take her animal away. She jerked away from him and gave him a dirty look. They weren't that familiar. Not anymore.

Kane swallowed hard and looked sick. Welcome

to the fucking club.

"Why are you here, Kiera? Do you need something from me? Some kind of help? Name it, and I'll do anything."

"Why would you help me now?" she said bitterly, yanking her gaze away from him and giving it to the woods again as she leaned up against her ride. "Don't you know it's too late?"

"You can get her back," Kane whispered, drawing up to her and grasping her shoulders. "I got mine back. Rowan bit me, and The Darkness was there. He had been all along. I just needed a claiming mark to release him."

"A claiming mark like this?" Kiera asked, pulling the neck of her sweater to the side to expose the four puncture wounds Justin had given her. They were her greatest shame. Those scars were from a desperation to be made whole by someone who was so very broken.

Seconds stretched on as Kane stared at her scars, shaking his head in denial. The proof was there, though. What had worked for him and Rowan hadn't worked for her. "My lioness is really gone. I've accepted it. Not easily, mind you, but I'm getting by. I guess I'm just here because I wanted some kind of connection to the life I had before she was taken from me."

"Me?"

"Yeah. Everyone from my old life is gone. I haven't seen anyone from Apex, and then you come up on the news and you have him again. You have the dragon. I was sitting there watching you battle with your mate, spewing fire like you used to, and I was just… I guess I wanted to see you for myself." Her eyes were burning with weak tears again, so she sniffed and kicked at the gravel. "I hate you, Kane. I hate that you got yours back, and I couldn't make it happen for mine." She looked up at him and gave him an emotional smile as tears streamed down her cheeks. "But I'm really, really happy for you."

Kane's eyes were full of heartache. He held out his hands, lips parted like he wanted to say something to fix this, but there was no such thing. There was no fix. There was just emptiness. He tried to pull her to him again, but she shook her head and stepped out of his reach. Kiera couldn't do another hug from her old friend right now without losing it completely. "It was good to see you again, Kane. Good luck with your crew."

"Don't leave, Kiera."

She forced her smile wider and gave him a two-fingered wave. "Later, Cowboy." She'd told him that the day they'd taken her from Apex after she'd been "cured." That was all she could think of to say goodbye, and it seemed fitting to say it again now. She wouldn't ever see him again after this.

And then, just like Beast had done, she climbed into her car and drove off as fast as she could without looking back.

TWO

Beast slammed on the brakes. His Raptor skidded at an angle until he came to a rocking stop on the shoulder of the winding mountain road. He was running. Always fucking running now. It's why he hadn't turned in his registration paperwork for the Blackwings. He'd given himself this beautiful out when shit got hard, and look what happened. It wasn't the D-Team that had driven him away. It was some broken former shifter with gorgeous lioness eyes frozen in her face. A lioness! No wonder she'd been calling to his damn rutting animal. It was the way she looked that had made it so fun to watch her watching the D-Team. Her eyes, so striking, so much like those in his pride. His pride, his pride, his fucking dead pride! Beast roared and slammed his open palm against the steering wheel over and over until he could breathe again.

Female fuckin' lion in his territory—of course his broken animal was hunting her. Kiera was all sick and pitiful and so goddamned beautiful he'd jacked off to her a dozen times since she'd slunk into his territory. He wished he could rip the memory of her beautiful face from his mind. Now that he knew what she was, he wanted nothing in the world to do with her. Why? Because every lion around him died. That was the curse. Didn't matter if hers had been stripped out of her body in that godforsaken cleansing facility, she was lioness enough. Her eye color said as much. How could he not have put it together? It was like his lion had blinded him to what she was, but why?

Because I wanted to keep her.

"You can't fucking keep her! You can't keep anything!" His throat hurt from the yell that had scratched up his throat. He should leave until she was long gone from Kane's Mountains.

Coward.

Beast huffed a hate-filled laugh and shook his head. Cowardly lion, that was rich. He bit the corner of his thumbnail and growled. That woman, Kiera—she was sick. And not just sick from her animal being stripped. There was something more. Head sick, heart sick, body sick—something was making her smell all wrong.

Dark hair, a deep plum color in the sun, spilling down her shoulders like she was a fucking dream. Dark eyebrows perfectly arched, her make-up flawless, tall, lithe, curves for days. But pale skin and a weak, hunched appearance that said she had some human sickness. Incurable maybe. Why else would she be hunting Kane, her old friend, if not to say goodbye?

Beast had been an asshole to her, but that couldn't be helped. It was better than getting her killed. It was better than cursing her. She would've thanked him if she knew who he was.

For the first time in two years, since the murder of his pride, he felt like talking to someone. He felt like unburdening himself just to see if it took some of the ache away. He would never, but still, the urge was there.

It was the damn D-Team's fault. He'd wanted to join Kane's crew because the scary-ass dragon would supposedly stay strong and rule from afar. Instead, he'd put together a crew of shifters who like to air their shit all the time. Beast wished everyone would just shut up and deal with their issues behind closed doors. This drive to relieve himself with a listening ear was all their fault.

He glared at the sign beside his truck. *Now Leaving Bryson City*. That had been the plan the second the word had slipped from her perfectly puckered lips. *Lioness*. This was his nightmare. The whole reason he'd come here in the first place was no freakin' lions, and then who shows up not three months after he applied for Kane's crew?

Coward.

"Shut the fuck up," he muttered to his inner animal as he pulled a U-Turn and headed back to Kane's Mountains.

He didn't want to run from the small sanctuary he'd found. Where else would he find an alpha big and bad enough to put him down when his animal dragged him into insanity? Nowhere. He needed the D-Team to keep him in check, and he would need Kane to protect the world from him when the time came.

Besides, Kiera was probably gone by now. He'd seen it in her eyes. She was a leaver just like him. That woman had one foot out of these mountains already. All he had to do was wait it out in the safety of his trailer until Kane gave him the okay to come out again.

The dragon knew the real story behind Beast's fall from power. He wouldn't make him face Kiera. He *wouldn't*. Beast was crew, and Kiera was sick.

She was ashes in the wind.

THREE

Kiera huffed an angry breath and turned away from her El Camino for the third time. Why was leaving the Smoky Mountains this hard?

She marched back into her motel room and let the door click closed behind her. Her reflection in the mirror made her sad. She looked as sick as she felt. Tired and weak. She hadn't slept well in years. Not since her lioness was taken. Now she had a constant feeling of restlessness. Like there was something she was supposed to be doing, something she couldn't remember.

Biting her bottom lip, she pulled the duffle bag strap over her head and settled it onto the made bed. The comforter was impeccable except for the indentation the bag made—the only proof of her being here. She liked to travel light, like a ghost.

Usually she ripped her gaze away from her reflection, but she needed to own this. She needed to remind herself of why she'd come here in the first place. There was a full-length mirror hanging from the bathroom door, and she gave it her profile, frowning at her loose sweater and baggy jeans. With a steadying breath, she lifted her shirt and cupped the swell of her belly. There was an instant fluttering there, like butterfly wings against her insides.

She would make the worst mother.

What could she provide this baby? She was a roaming cocktail waitress who paid for hotels and rental properties with tips from rich guys who liked to stare at her ass in tight clothes. And right now, she couldn't even do that job because she was four months pregnant, and unless clients had prego-fetishes, she wasn't the body type anymore.

This baby wouldn't be a fake human like her, no. This baby would be a lion shifter like its father. Fucking Justin. All she'd wanted was a meaningless claiming mark so she could get her animal back, but he'd negotiated terms. He'd drawn it out, demanded sex for the bite, and she'd given in time and time again, because he always acted like he would give her the bite during each coupling. He'd planned this, hadn't used protection no matter how much she'd asked him too, and now in hindsight she could see everything so clear. This had been his plan. He thought the bite was going to work too, and if he got her pregnant, he thought she would step into his pride and pledge everlasting fealty like his other lionesses. He would've been the alpha to bring a rogue to her knees. Well, screw his plans. Now she was on the run, hoping with a bone-deep desperation that he didn't find her. She would be damned if she let this baby be raised in his awful pride.

She couldn't protect it alone, so the best thing she could do for the child she carried would be to give it to the dragons. Just the thought of parting with this little life inside of her made her eyes burn with emotion though. Even sick and weak, she wished the pregnancy would stretch on and on so she could keep this little piece of happiness. Even though she was going through hell, she wasn't alone. She had someone to think of more than herself and that got her through the dark days.

Kiera sniffed hard and settled her shirt back over her stomach, then lay on the bed like a starfish and stared at the ceiling fan. When the fluttering intensified into a rolling sensation, she rested her hand there to see if she could feel the movement from the outside yet. She'd never wanted her lioness back as badly as when she'd taken those four at-home pregnancy tests. A huge part of her wished she had that strength back to raise the cub herself. But what kind of a life could she give a shifter when there was no chance of ever being a shifter again herself? Every time the baby Changed, it would break her heart.

But…

She loved the idea that this baby meant there was a little bit of lion in her right now. She liked imagining she wasn't too broken to raise it outside of a pride. Sometimes she even pretended she could keep it. She already loved it so much she'd quit drinking, quit all the bad habits she'd been partaking in. Her old life had been wild and out of control, but now, her thoughts were consumed by doing what was best for the baby. If not for this tiny, fragile life inside of her, she would've never come to the mountains of the dark dragon.

Oh, she remembered Kane. Kane as a boy had been kind, protective even. Kane as a dragon was a monster. In Apex, she'd lived with the fear that they would not only succeed in taking her animal, but that Kane would burn the facility to the ground with her in it. Death by fire terrified her, yet here she was, facing the dragon again.

Kiera rolled onto her side and cradled her belly. She would do anything to give the baby a good home, but not with a pride. If it was a girl, she would be one of many mates to a dominant male. If it was a boy, he would be raised to breed many and connect with none. He would be raised a brawler. He would likely die young in fights to keep a pride. She needed the dragons to take the baby and protect it from Justin and all of his powerful allies because Kiera couldn't. She was rogue without the ability to call on her animal to keep her child safe. Justin would find her, find her child, and he would kill her without a single thought if it meant he could keep his offspring. Cubs meant power and virility. Cubs kept Justin king over his domain. And Kiera would do anything to keep her child from being a number in his awful Tarian Pride.

Rumor had it Rowan wouldn't be able to survive

birthing a full-blooded baby dragon. Rumor also had it the dragons were searching for surrogates and possible adoptions. Rowan could survive by raising a little lion cub.

The complication? One badass, murderous, dominant-as-hell alpha lion named Beast. If he was as bad as everyone said, he was more animal than man and would kill another male's offspring in his territory.

If she was going to stay here and feel out whether Kane's Mountains would be a good home for her cub, she needed to hide this pregnancy. And beyond that, she needed to chase away the Beast. There was still time since he hadn't officially registered to the Blackwing Crew.

She had to make sure he would never come back and harm her cub.

****

Beast pulled his truck to a stop in his side yard and narrowed his eyes at the dunce on his front porch. What the fuck did Dustin want?

It had already been an infinitely long day, Beast was caked in sweat from working at the gem mine Kane had just bought, his muscles ached, his head throbbed, and yeah, his dick was still throbbing, too, because apparently his stupid lion couldn't let go of the vision of Kiera's perfect fucking lips and tits. He really liked her purple hair and that cute little nose ring that looked like a tiny piece of glitter in the sun, and *aaaah!*

He didn't want to deal with the mouthy wolf right now. He just wanted to drink himself into oblivion and maybe shift later and kill stuff. Dustin would be fun to hunt.

Beast snarled and shoved his truck door open. "I knew you were dumb, wolf," he murmured, pointing to the No Trespassing sign he'd posted on the fence around his singlewide trailer. "But I didn't know you were that dumb."

"Flattery will get you everywhere with me, friend."

"We're not friends," Beast muttered, kicking the gate open. He strode toward his porch. "Fuck off."

"See, I disagree, on account of you saving my life. Remember? I was being slowly bled to death by three packs." Dustin held three fingers up like Beast was the dumb one. He wanted to bite off his hand.

"And then here comes my ride-or-die lady and

one scary-ass lion to help me out of that little jam. I'm still knockin' boots with Emma thanks to you." Dustin stretched his legs out from Beast's green porch chair, bought on sale for two bucks at the grocery store. Stupid Dustin was going to make it smell like wolf farts. Beast curbed the urge to chuck Dustin, along with the chair, over the fence.

Irritated, he pointed to the black folder on Dustin's lap, the one the wolf obviously wanted him to notice since he was pelvic thrusting it up in the air. "What's that?" Beast wanted to sleep for a week, but this was a crew, and apparently he was supposed to make an effort with them.

"What this?" Dustin asked innocently.

Games. Beast rolled his eyes heavenward and yanked open the door of his trailer. "Bye, Dustin."

But Dustin followed directly, as if he wanted to die today.

Beast rounded on him. "My territory, get out."

"Kiera is still here."

Well, that felt like a kick to the gonads. His heart sank to the laminate flooring under his feet. "What?"

"Kane was acting all sketchy, and have you noticed? Logan ain't around. He's been MIA for two days."

"Yeah, well, he has a job now, one that doesn't include killing people, so fucking good for him."

"Yeah, he has that one, and the job Kane gave him."

Beast narrowed his eyes. He thought he was Kane's right-hand man. Kane always came to him first seeking advice with problems. Why? Because he'd done this alpha shit for ten years and knew how to navigate treacherous waters while the dark dragon was still a new alpha. One who sometimes barely liked his crew. Mostly because of Dustin. "What job?"

"Perhaps you should sit down for this," Dustin said innocently. He wore a dumb grin as though savoring the stupid secret he was holding.

"Spill it or I'll kill you," Beast said nonchalantly as he walked to the fridge and pulled out a beer.

"Empty threats."

False. Beast really did want to kill Dustin three dozen times a day and sometimes more. Same with Logan. Same with Kane, same with any male in his territory, thanks to his broken lion. Females were the only ones truly safe from him. Kane should probably put him down now. Or maybe Logan would do it since that was his old job—putting down sick shifters. He'd probably enjoy it. He and Logan fought like animals any time they were around each other.

"You get lost in your head a lot for a dude," Dustin said, twirling the folder on one finger.

Beast glared at the werewolf and chugged his beer. Dustin spoke the truth, but fuck him for pointing it out.

"Logan's watching Kiera."

What those three words did to his insides. Beast squeezed the bottle so hard, it shattered in his hands, and a long slice across his palm starting pouring blood. "Shit," he muttered, wrapping it in a hand towel. Now he was good and pissed, so he wrenched his voice up to yelling. "What do you mean he's watching her? Not hunting her. Not stalking her. Don't fucking tell me he's after a kill. She ain't a shifter, and fuck him for following her, and fuck Kane for caring."

"Fuck Kane for caring? You just threw a tantrum because someone else is *looking* at her."

"Because I don't like Logan stalking a woman. He's a mercenary—"

"Ex-mercenary—"

"What, you think he dropped the instinct to hunt? To kill sick shifters?"

"You said she wasn't a shifter."

Now Dustin was messing with him. Twisting words and making him speak in circles, and he wasn't doing this shit. Three steps to Dustin, and Beast moved to wrap his hand around his throat to get him to stop talking.

At the last moment, Dustin held up a folder that Beast accidentally grabbed instead. The shitty handwriting on the front read *Kiera Pierce*.

Dustin ducked out of pawing range and jammed a finger at the folder. "I know you don't want her here, but there are too many secrets in this crew. Like why the fuck weren't we told Kiera is still in the territory? You I get, but they are leaving me and Emma out of their little secret stalk, too. I snuck in Kane's house today while you two were at work and found this."

"What is it?" Beast asked, his voice more animal than man right now. He hated when he got this riled up, hated the gravel to his tone.

"That's everything Kane dug up on Kiera. You know as well as I do the dragon knows everything about everyone, and he's got tons of dirt on this one. She's a total nutcase, Beast." Dustin snarled up his lip. "And you know what Kane does with total nutcases."

Beast heaved a sigh. "Yeah. He makes them Blackwings." He looked suspiciously at Dustin and held up the black folder. "Why did you give this to me?"

"Because like it or not, I really do consider you a friend. I owe you for going to battle with me against the packs. You showed up first, and that counts for something big with me. You freaked the fuck out yesterday when you found out Kiera was a lioness. I don't know why, but I saw the panic in your eyes, and I don't want you to leave the Blackwings. Not because of Kiera, not because of anything." Dustin made his way to the door, but turned just before he left and made an elaborate sign with his hands. He'd been learning American Sign Language for his hearing-impaired mate. "Emma says I should be more open with my feelings. Do you know what I just said to you?"

"I don't care."

"I said I love you, too, because I know deep down you—"

"Get out before I kill you."

"Yep, see you later," Dustin rushed out with a nod, then disappeared out the front door.

Beast really, really didn't like the idea of Logan tailing Kiera. Or that she was still in the territory. Or that Kane was keeping secrets from Beast. He'd been Kane's confidant in the crew—the one Kane came to for advice. He'd been the one Kane had tasked with finding out what Dustin was really up to when he was thinking of betraying their crew to the Valdoro pack. Honestly, right now Beast felt a little demoted. Maybe Kane was going to make Logan his Third.

Beast looked down at the folder. He had respect for dark pasts and really shouldn't read this. Kiera wasn't offering it, so it was like he was stealing her secrets, and something about that curdled his stomach. The folder made a slapping sound as it hit the table. Without a look back at it, Beast peeled off his shirt and strode for the bathroom where he was going to shower and refuse to jerk off for the freaking second time today while thinking about that sexy ex-lioness. Maybe she was in heat or something. Maybe that's why his animal was going mad for her. Or maybe he was just so damn deprived after running a pride for ten years and taking care of the females in heat. They required sex multiple times a day, and going from that to nothing had shocked his system. He wasn't like this with the other females in the crew at all, but Kiera had him rutting so freaking hard. Probably because of those pretty lioness eyes. And her curves. And her little nose, rosy cheeks, and her hair all piled up, making him want to yank out the hair band and run his fingers through her long locks, flip her over on a bed, and fuck her from behind while gripping that pretty purple hair and...crap. Now he was hard again.

For that little fantasy, he deserved a cold shower, and that was just what he got. He ignored the hell out of his raging boner because he had to get this under control. He felt like a freaking addict right now.

Dustin had said there was dirt on Kiera in that folder, so maybe that was the solution. Maybe if he read all the terrible things about her, he would be so turned off it would cure whatever was happening to his body.

Mind made up and moral compass smashed to smithereens, he wrapped a towel around his hips and strode into the kitchen, flipped open the folder, and yanked out the contents. A medical bracelet fell onto the table. It was splattered with dark brown spots, and when Beast lifted it to his nose and sniffed, he wanted to retch. It was old blood.

Kiera Rain Pierce, age 15, lioness, not to be left unattended. There was a logo on the underside of the bracelet. Apex.

Beast sat slowly in the chair and read the first page. It was a letter written in a kid's scribbled handwriting. All the *B*s were backward. Across the top it read *Kiera age 9*.

When I grow up I want to be a police woman or maybe a firefighter so I can help people. Henry said girls can't be firefighters but I'm a lion shifter. I'm strong. I could get in and out of houses really fast and carry people to safety. My mom is a firefighter and she is the strongest person in the world.

Underneath, there was a picture done in crayon of two lionesses, a big one and a small one sitting next to each other. There was a house and flowers in the background with a rainbow across the top of them.

Jesus. A huge part of him didn't even want to know what happened to her. He had enough of his own shit to deal with.

The next page was an official looking document with the Apex logo across the top.

Kiera is showing signs of success. We almost lost her last week, but she recovered and this morning wasn't able to Change. We thought she was lying to us again, but when she was prodded with electricity, she was truly unable to defend herself. We aren't there yet, but we're getting closer with her. I think this one will live.

Beast's hands shook as he barely resisted the urge to crumple the paper and burn it to ashes. He hated Apex with the fire of a million suns. Kane was just now pulling out of what they'd done to him, and Beast constantly saw the cracks in the dragon's façade. Kiera would never get the chance to recover. She never got her animal back like Kane did.

There was a Ziploc bag with pictures. Beast pulled them out carefully. They were all out of order. That bothered him, so he spread them out and put them right. There was one of Kiera probably around the age she drew the picture of her and her mom.

Sandy-blond hair, bangs in her big blue eyes, hair all curled and in pigtails, two missing front teeth. Cute kid. It was a school picture, and she was sitting up straight. She looked happy. Normal. Her shirt read *Teachers Rule*. Beast smiled. He couldn't help himself. She was probably the class brownnoser. He could imagine her sitting at the front of the class and raising her hand as fast as she could every time the teacher asked a question.

There were pictures of her on a soccer team, one of her in a cheerleading uniform being thrown up in the air. Next was a selfie. She was standing in front of a mirror in a black dress, dead eyes locked on the camera, cheeks and nose red as though she'd been crying. She was maybe fourteen.

Beast rushed through the rest of the pictures, all apparently from Apex. He couldn't look at those for too long. Kiera was like a corpse. Sometimes her eyes were blue, and sometimes one was gold. The ones where she was emaciated, her head was shaved, showing three deep surgical scars on the side. In those, her eyes were dead and frozen in that lioness color.

Kane had once shown him a similar picture of

himself when Beast had asked about Apex.

There was a tattered newsprint obituary for her mom. Firefighting accident. Burning building her mom hadn't been able to escape. She died saving a little boy. Apparently Kiera had some hero in her bloodlines.

Next was a list of names Kane had put together.

Holly Dunes – lion, killed in transition

Brandon Fastmen – wolf, killed in transition

Meghan Stewart – grizzly bear, killed in transition

Dawn Evener – grizzly bear, no trace of animal, married, two human children

Kannon Dayton – wolf, deceased, took life

Kiera Pierce – lion, no trace of animal, never married, never registered to a pride, no children

Caleb Porter – panther, killed in transition

Ben Porter – panther, last seen in Bilk Creek Mountains. On the move. In hiding. Married. Mated? Animal? One child. Human? Shifter? No established contact.

Where the fuck are you, Ben?

LSKDJFLSKJFDLKF

Kane had found Ben only recently. And now he'd

found Kiera.

No animal, never married, never registered to a pride, no children, and hell, he was having a really hard time hating her now. She'd lost so much. Perhaps she'd even lost as much as Beast. He never thought he would find someone as irreparably damaged as him, and yet here was this woman who was now sick, without her animal, and completely rogue. Of course she'd never registered with a pride. Prides weren't like crews. They didn't accept humans, and that's how they would've seen Kiera. She had no shot of joining up with other lions. She either had to join a crew, which she clearly didn't do, or join the human world that had stripped her animal from her.

He didn't know Kiera, but something deep inside of him told him that after her mom died, she had never fit in again. Back when he was alpha, back when he was okay, back when he was king, he would've taken her into his pride, even as a human.

Beast frowned. But then she would be dead.

He couldn't read this shit anymore, so he shoved everything back in the folder and slapped it closed.

The thought of Logan watching her hotel room drew a deep rumble up his throat. He wanted to gut that bear for hunting her, and he didn't really give a single fuck that Kane had ordered Logan to do it. Kiera was a lioness, or she had been once. This wasn't Logan's business.

Beast made his way into his room and dressed as fast as he could. Since his chest was still wet from the shower, it made dark spots all over his black sweater, but so what? No one looked at him like he was fuckable. More like a monster instead. He snarled when he caught his reflection in the bathroom mirror. Stupid face all torn to hell, a constant reminder of what had happened. No wonder Kiera had smelled scared of him.

She was a beauty. He was a beast.

He needed to chase Logan away. No, wait. He was supposed to chase Kiera away. From the mountains, from Kane's territory...from *his* territory. But that didn't feel right anymore. Stupid protective instincts had confused him for a minute, but he was getting his head back on straight little by little. He just had to ignore the pictures he saw. If she stayed here, near him, he would ruin her life even more. And a huge part of him wanted Kiera to be all right now. To be a success story. To get her act together, find her strength, and heal from whatever was making her smell sick.

Beast grabbed his coat and winter hat and shoved the door open. He didn't even bother turning off the lights in his trailer before he bolted down the porch steps and through the gate to his truck.

"You're welcome," Dustin called from his front porch swing where he was cuddling with Emma under a thick blanket.

Asshole. Beast flipped him off as he drove by. And furthermore, they were a disgusting couple, always cuddling everywhere. Kissing and slow blinking at each other like they were in a damn romantic movie. *I'll love you for eternity* and all that horse-crap. Love wasn't real, but Dustin and Emma liked to pretend. So did Logan and Winter, so did Kane and Rowan. It was puke-inducing.

When Beast gassed it over the bridge, his lion reared up inside of him at the prospect of fighting Logan. It had been two whole days since they'd bled each other.

And for some reason Beast couldn't understand, Kiera felt like the perfect reason to sharpen his claws on some bear hide.

FOUR

Kiera pushed the curtain aside and glared at the beat-up white truck in the next parking lot over. At least she still had impeccable vision from the cat. She was being hunted by Logan Furrow of the Blackwings, but why?

Oh, she knew what he was—a mercenary. But she wasn't a shifter, and killing her would bring down hell on Kane's Mountains. No way would she go quietly. Not now. Not with a life to protect.

For two days, he'd followed her. Sometimes his mate, Winter, came with him, sometimes not. He talked on his phone sometimes. He had to be better at hunting than this, but she'd grown suspicious he must not care about being caught.

Was he here to push her out of the mountains? To make sure she really left like Beast had ordered her to? Or was his reasoning more sinister?

Not one to pussyfoot around, she slid the bowie knife from her bag into the back of her jeans and pulled her sweater over it. Then, with a three-count breath for bravery, she marched across the motel parking lot and into the adjacent lot of Frankie's Burgers & Tots.

Mouth full of burger, Logan rolled down his window. Around the bite, he said, "About damn time."

"You've been following me for two days. Why?"

He gulped. "Good instincts still. And because Kane told me to. He's alpha, so I do what he says."

"Bullshit, you're as dominant as he is. Even I can feel how fucked up you are. You could say no if you wanted."

"Nope, he really is alpha. Doesn't matter how broken my animal is. I still don't want to end up in the belly of the dragon. Tater tot?" He handed her a carton half full of the fried potatoes.

She was always hungry, sooo... "Thanks," she muttered, yanking them from his hand and taking three steps back to eat them.

"It's cold, and you don't have a jacket," he said, dark eyebrows arched high as he took another bite of burger.

"What do you care?"

"About you? My care-level is at maybe three percent. Nah, it's what you got hidden in your belly that has me concerned."

Kiera nearly choked on the tot she was devouring. She coughed a few times and bullied it down her throat. "I don't know what you mean."

"And neither do any of the other Blackwings, as far as I can tell. Clearly they've never been around a pregnant lady because they just keep talking about how sick you smell. You don't smell sick, though. You smell fertilized."

"Gross. That's a seriously gross way to put it." Kiera looked around to make sure they were truly alone. "I don't really want it known."

"Hey," Logan said, throwing up his hands. "When you announce your bundle of joy is up to you. I haven't said anything."

Kiera narrowed her eyes. "Why not? They're your crew."

He canted his head and frowned. "I don't know

exactly. Instinct? If I told them, would you run?"

"Maybe."

Logan nodded slowly. "Well, I have orders to keep you in the territory, so that would just make my job harder. Your secret is safe with me."

The chilly breeze kicked up, so Kiera wrapped her arms around herself to keep warm. Shifting her weight from side-to-side, she admitted, "You're the first person I've talked to about this, and you're a total stranger."

Logan shrugged. "It's the easiest way to talk about stuff." She opened her mouth to say more, but he put his hand up and rushed out, "Not that I want to hear about it. I don't. I just want you to stay in the mountains so Kane doesn't burn my ass."

"Right. Well, you can stop following me, at least until the end of the week. I told the guy at the front desk I'm staying through Friday."

"John?" he asked. "Nice guy. I still have to tail you, though. You know, you could make this a lot easier by talking to Kane. He doesn't want to lose track of you again, but he's trying to give you your space—"

"By having me followed."

Logan gave her an empty smile and continued. "If it was up to him, he would storm the motel and drag you back to his mountains, but he has a mate with a sensitive soul, and Rowan doesn't want you feeling pressured. She wants you to have a chance to come when you're ready."

That bit of information drew Kiera up straighter. Kane had found a good mate then. One who could take the edge off him. Kiera touched her belly gently. That was good news.

"Why hasn't Beast registered to the crew yet?" She'd tried but failed for nonchalance if Logan's suspicious little slits for eyes were anything to go by.

"If you're after the Beast, best go looking for love elsewhere. Even the dark dragon is wary of him, and for good reason."

"Because he's dangerous?"

"Yeah. To any male in the territory."

Kiera rubbed her chilled arms and kicked a loose rock on the asphalt. "But not females?"

"Nope. The females are safe. He's got a dominance problem, though. Mountains aren't exactly a safe haven if you have a dick, if you know what I mean."

Actually, she didn't know what he meant. He'd murdered his pride, all females. That's probably where he got that hideous scar down his face. Fuckin' deserved it.

"You've eaten all the tater tots," Logan pointed out.

Kiera looked down at the empty carton and swallowed the last bite. "Yeah, I'm still hungry so I'm going to go get some dinner." She walked toward Frankie's, but called over her shoulder, "Please stop following me."

"No can do." Logan went back to eating another burger.

Geez, she missed her lioness metabolism. She'd forgotten how much shifters could eat in one sitting.

The word "fuck" echoed across the parking lot, and Logan's engine flared to life. Kiera turned to see a blue Ford Raptor turning in.

Logan called out, "Sorry, Cat-Woman, I'm not up for a row tonight." Whatever that meant.

After Logan peeled out of the parking lot, Beast parked in his place. He didn't get out, though, just sat behind the wheel and trapped her with his sparking gold eyes. Why was he so riled up that his animal was this close to the surface? She hadn't done anything wrong.

Or maybe he was the one hunting her now. A shiver blasted up her spine, so she jogged into Frankie's and out from under his glare. Surely he wouldn't go murder-kitty in a public place. She was safe here. Probably.

She ordered her food, but when she turned around, the only tables available were against the front window. Being in Beast's direct view would've been nerve-wracking enough, but as she made her way to the table in the middle, Beast strode toward her across the parking lot.

He wore a black sweater that clung to his perfectly defined shoulders and chest. It tapered at the waist, giving him a delicious V-shape that caused her mouth to plop open. He was jogging, hands shoved in his pockets so that his dark jeans hung low on his hips. A strip of stomach was exposed, and even from here, in the dim light of evening, she could see the muscles over his hips that delved into his pants. His face was turned, as if his attention was on the motel, his flawless side on display. Beast could've been a model if not for the scars on the other side.

He pulled the door open and locked gazes with her. There was a moment where they just stood there, looking at each other from across the restaurant. His breath came quicker. He rubbed his hands together as if he was cold. His eyes were the bright gold of his people. Of the people she used to be a part of. She was shocked again by how tall he was, how broad shouldered...how handsome despite the marred left side of his face.

Beautiful man, ruined soul.

Before he moved toward the counter with supernatural grace, he angled his face away from her, exposed his neck ever so slightly. Why would he do that? She was no threat to him. She was no threat to anyone. The oxygen had been sucked right out of the room. She sat slowly on the edge of the seat, perched carefully for an escape.

Twice while he was ordering, Beast turned his profile toward her, as if he was looking at her with his peripheral. He was careful not to make eye contact, though, as he took a table three down from hers. No one was between them, so they sat there, watching each other from the edges of their vision, ignoring each other, and ignoring the lightning-like electric currents that zinged through the air between them.

Warmth pooled deep in her belly. What was happening?

The ding of the entry doorbell dragged her out of her trance. Kane walked in, eyes green with those elongated dragon pupils like he was worked up, too. He gave the back of Beast's head a death glare, but Beast responded to him before he even saw the dragon.

"I'm not here to chase her off."

"The fuck you are."

"How did you know I was here?"

"Dustin stole something from me." Kane's voice shook with rage. "He's got it in his head he wants to be your friend, so I can guess what he did with it." Kane loudly pulled a metal chair away from a newly vacated table right near Beast's booth, sat in the chair backward, and finally, finally, gave Kiera his attention.

Kane still looked mad as hell, and the faint scent of smoke filled the air as his glowing eyes locked on hers. "You okay?"

Beast made a ticking sound behind his teeth and

leaned back in his bench seat. "She's in no danger from me, and you know it."

"I don't want her pushed out."

"I'm not pushing her out!"

"What's going on?" Kiera asked, utterly baffled.

"Go on, tell her, Beast. Why are you here?"

Beast gritted his teeth so hard his chiseled jaw twitched. He shook his head, denying Kane, but his eyes never left Kiera.

"Tell her!" Kane snapped, power slamming through his words. "Why are you here?"

"Because I can't stop thinking about her." The words came out choked, as if Kane had dragged them from Beast's throat. His cheeks turned red, and he stared out the window. His fists were clenched on the table.

Kane's face changed completely. In an instant, the anger disappeared, morphed into confusion, and then settled into realization. "What?" he asked low.

"You fuckin' heard me, *Alpha*."

There was a loaded moment between the two brawlers, then Kane stood in a rush and looked at Kiera. The dragon had left his eyes to leave them soft brown, like the Kane she'd seen in Apex. "I'm sorry. I shouldn't have come." He made to leave but hesitated by Beast. He ran his hands down his dark whiskers and murmured, "Beast—"

"Don't." Beast twitched his head and kept his gaze on the window.

Kane swallowed hard and turned to Kiera. "Please come see me tomorrow. Come to my mountains. Talk to me. I'm asking you as a friend not to leave until you can convince me you're okay. I won't be able to stop looking for you again if you don't."

"Okay," she murmured.

And then Kane left without a look back. He strode across the darkening parking lot, got into his Bronco, and pulled away. Surely, he wouldn't leave her here with Beast if he thought she was in danger…right?

"Number one-sixty-five and one-sixty-six," a bored-sounding teenager said over the intercom.

That was her, but when she stood to retrieve her food, Beast gestured for her to stay put and muttered, "I've got it."

When he set the tray down in front of her too hard, her burger bounced. He carried his own tray back to a table one closer to her. He didn't seem inclined to speak, but she had questions, so after a few minutes of munching in silence, Kiera moved one table closer to him, and now only one empty table separated them.

Beast cleared his throat and moved to that table, cast her a quick glance, inhaled deeply, and then went back to eating one of his three hamburgers and mini Mount Everest of tater tots.

Kiera was drawn to him. She wanted so badly to sit across from him while they ate. She didn't mind quiet. Her life had been bathed in it, and Beast seemed like a man of few words. What she did mind, though, was the lingering fact he was a murderer.

"You smell scared," he said, his voice low and growly. He wasn't meeting her eyes, but she could see a bit of the color of his every once in a while, and they weren't human.

"I know who you are."

"Nobody knows who I am."

"You're Beast of the Calamity Pride."

He ghosted her a glance and huffed a breath. His lip snarled up. "So you know my name. Doesn't mean you know anything about me."

"Alpha ten years, from age eighteen to twenty-eight. Your pride had twelve females in it—"

"Stop," he demanded.

"One of the biggest prides in North America. You were a legend—"

"I said *stop*," he uttered louder, sitting up straight.

"—until you murdered your entire pride," she gritted out. He should fucking know she wasn't some prey he could follow around. She wasn't the hunted. She'd been through hell and back and wasn't about to fall victim to some serial killer in a pretty package.

Beast snarled out a terrifying sound, eyes locked on something out the window. In a blur, he stood, chucked his food in the trash, and then bolted out the door. He ran his hand roughly back and forth over his short hair as he jogged to his truck. At the door, he turned back around, his face so full of pain it hurt to look at him. Chest heaving, he locked his gaze with hers and scrubbed his hand down his dark blond facial scruff. He yanked the door open to his Raptor and pulled out a notebook. He bit off the lid of a permanent marker and spit it into the car, then scribbled something as he strode back toward the window. When he reached it, he slammed the notebook against the glass, right in front of her face.

You don't know me. No one does. You're wrong.

"About what?" she asked.

"Everything," he barked through the glass, his eyes flashing with such conviction it stole her breath. He walked away, his furious golden gaze lingering on her over his shoulder. And then he loaded up into his Raptor, and spun out of the parking lot.

I can't stop thinking about her.

Kane had forced the truth from the titan lion. Perhaps he wasn't hunting her. Perhaps he was as curious about her as she was about him.

She was wrong about everything? Every rumor she'd ever heard about Beast had painted him as a monster, but now she wasn't so sure. He'd been hurt when she mentioned what had happened. His body had been shaking. This whole time, she'd thought Kane had made a misstep by letting a true killer into his crew, but Kane was smart. He always had been, and clearly devoted to his mate. What reason would he have to let someone who murdered an entire pride into his crew?

Unless…

Perhaps Beast wasn't the beast she imagined at all.

The red glow of his taillights disappeared into the evening shadows.

This was the second time he'd run away, and she was just as baffled by him this time as the last.

FIVE

Kiera pulled to a stop at the very top of the road that led down into the valley of Kane's Mountains. It was such a steep drop-off, she couldn't see the road in front of the nose of her El Camino. She just had to trust that the gravel lane was there.

Trust wasn't her forte. Never had been, and this leap into the unknown felt like a parallel to trusting Kane. If she went another inch further, she would be in the dragon's territory and skidding down a road that wouldn't let her escape quickly.

It was a moment of commitment. She would let Kane in. She would give into her curiosity about Beast. She would risk exposing her pregnancy to get closer to these broken shifters.

But that was the point, right? To ask for help, to seek comfort, to talk to someone...to live.

Kiera eased onto the gas and then coasted down the steep gravel road, foot hovering over the brake until it leveled out. The single lane wound through towering trees. It was January, and most had dropped their leaves, covering the ground in a thick blanket. She gassed it over a bridge, but hesitated at a split in the road. Both were worn and used often; one was gravel, one dirt. Through the bare trees to the right, she could make out a sign, but the words were covered by tree limbs. The gravel road curved off to the left, and behind a grove of trees lifted a plume of chimney smoke. It was as if the dragons were beckoning her.

Kiera pulled the wheel to the left and followed the winding loose-pebble road until it led her to a clearing with a modest cabin. Relieved she'd come late enough in the day that he wasn't still at work, she parked beside Kane's Bronco.

The storm clouds above were churning a deep gray color. She hugged her baggy white sweater tighter to her chest. Today she wore leggings and knee-high riding boots. She didn't know why she'd dressed up. Well...that was a lie. She'd dressed up on the off-chance she would run into Beast in these mountains. Shame heated her cheeks. Her heart had the worst taste in men, but since last night, when the rawness in Beast's eyes had told her she was wrong about him, she couldn't get him out of her mind. The way he moved so gracefully for a big behemoth of a man, the way his shoulders stretched his shirt, the way his voice had sounded when he'd admitted he couldn't stop thinking about her. The way he'd seemed at war with himself before he'd fled last night, like he wanted to leave, but couldn't until she understood the truth about him.

She'd slept badly last night replaying every moment she'd spent with him—which were few—and every word he'd said. Replaying every rumor and trying to match them up with the man she'd seen before her.

Clearly, Kiera was losing her mind. She was focusing on something interesting perhaps to escape the hard decision that lay ahead. This morning she'd woken up wanting more than anything to keep the baby. Some days were like this, but she'd read pamphlets on adoption, and they all said this was normal. The back-and-forth would likely happen until it came down to decision time. It was torture on her head and heart, so it made sense that both wanted to latch onto Beast and escape the hard parts of her life.

The breeze whipped her long curls around, so she brushed them behind her shoulder, lifted her fist, and wrapped her knuckles onto the wooden door.

There was murmuring coming from inside, but she didn't have the strong animal senses anymore and couldn't make out any words. No one answered, so she knocked again, stepped back, and rested on the porch railing to look out over Kane's Mountains. She would be hard-pressed to find a place as beautiful as this if she searched her whole life.

The door swung open, and there stood the man of her dreams himself. Beast filled up the entire doorway. Kiera froze like a stone and waited for her fear to make an appearance, but it didn't. Not when Beast had adverted his gaze and exposed his neck to her.

"I think I have to talk to you."

Kiera frowned. "Okay. But…how did you know I was here?"

"I can smell you, plus—" He jerked his chin to the

top corner of the porch where there was a small camera.

So getting the animal back didn't stop the paranoia. Her heart hurt for Kane. She dragged her attention back to Beast. "I think I have to talk to you, too."

Beast stumbled forward out of the doorway like someone had pushed him, and behind him, the door slammed closed. Okay then.

Beast straightened up to his full height and looked down at her, his eyes impassive, his hands clenched formally behind his back. He wore a white thermal sweater the same shade as hers over dirt-smeared hole-riddled jeans and scuffed-up work boots. His eyes looked so blue right now, like a spring sky. He hadn't shaved again, so his dirty blond beard was thicker today. Still didn't cover up the scars, not even close.

Beast made a tick sound behind his teeth and angled his scarred side away from her. "Don't like when people stare at them," he ground out.

She had to form this next question carefully because she wanted to know how to feel about those scars, and if she pried too hard, he would shut down on her. "Did you get them defending yourself?"

Beast shook his head.

Kiera cleared her throat delicately and tried again. "How did you get them?" Because if his answer was killing his pride, she was gone.

"Protecting my pride."

Such potent relief flooded through her, it almost buckled her knees. "I can still hear lies," she whispered, wringing her hands in front of her belly. "Am I in danger alone with you like this?"

Beast huffed a disgusted sound and shot her a dirty look. "No female has ever been in danger from me."

She waited until he didn't dance around the question.

"No," he said clearly, his voice trilling with honesty. "I would protect you, not hurt you."

"Do you want to take a walk with me? I came to see Kane—"

"Lie."

Kiera swallowed hard and tried again. "I came to see Kane and hoped to see you."

"Better. Yes. I will walk beside you." He said it oddly, though, like it was an oath.

Sometimes he said things strangely. He responded stiffly, and for some reason, it made her smile. His discomfort around people rivaled her own.

"You're laughing at me," he ground out as he led her down the porch stairs and toward the gravel road.

When Beast put a good ten feet between them, her smile deepened. "I'm not laughing at you. You remind me of me."

He cast her a confused frown. "You said you needed to talk to me."

Kiera nodded and stooped, picked up a stick from the middle of the road. "I wanted to apologize for making assumptions. I don't know your story. I listened to rumors, but rumors have hurt me before, too."

"How?"

Kiera dragged the end of the long, craggy stick along the gravel, creating a line as she walked. She was avoiding the hell out of his gaze because the lion looked at her as if he could see through her. It was unsettling, and especially now when she was going to give him something big. "My mom was rogue. I wasn't raised in a pride. The local pride made up whatever stories they wanted about how we lived. And when she died, those rumors made sure I wasn't taken in by them. My mom had a friend in there, a low-ranking female named Tammy. She'd wanted to adopt me as her own, but the alpha male and the other females wouldn't allow it. They thought I would taint the pride, taint the bloodlines. They thought I was from stock that couldn't function in a pride. I had a social worker. I called her Mrs. Lindsey, who was really nice, and she tried really hard to get the pride to take me in, but all those rumors about my mom and me stomped out that opportunity."

"And then you ended up in Apex."

Kiera's attention snapped to him.

He was walking with his hands still clenched behind his back, but only eight feet separated them now.

"I don't want to talk about that part," she said softly.

"You don't have to. I already know all about it."

Kiera put a couple extra feet in between them for that. It felt like a betrayal. "You checked up on me."

"Kane has your files. I read them. I didn't want to, but I thought if you were pitiful, I would think about you less."

She huffed a shocked breath. "And?"

"I think about you more." When a long snarl rattled his throat, Beast shook his head hard.

"Apex wasn't my choice, but it was the law at the time. Shifters that belonged to the state were given to Apex before they were allowed to be adopted by humans. And I'm not pitiful, Beast. I went through something hard, but I'm still here. Do you see tears in my eyes while I talk to you about this? Those stopped a long time ago."

"You cried when you saw Kane."

Anger pounded through her that he dared to point out her weakness. "I hated Kane, and I missed him terribly. Then I hated him, missed him, on and on and on. That was a hard moment you saw. I said I wasn't pitiful, not emotionless. I had a decent life after Apex. Did Kane's file have that? I got adopted three months after my lioness was taken, and by humans who were kind and who understood that I was going through hell. That I was missing a vital piece of me, a vital connection to my mom. They were always tender."

"I was raised by a gorilla shifter," he blurted out.

A long hiss sounded from him, and he took a long steadying inhale that stopped it. "Sorry. I'm not good at talking, and you smell angry now, or…disappointed?"

He'd shocked her so hard she'd dropped her stick. "Are you part gorilla?" That would explain his size and his ability to hold a pride for so long.

"No. My parents were both lions. Good at being lions, shit at being parents. But I got lucky. Got taken in by an old silverback who didn't have a family."

"What was his name?"

Beast's mouth curved up in a breathtaking smile, and his eyes softened as he chuckled. "Beast."

"Beast? Did he name you after him?"

Another deep, sexy laugh. "His real name is Callum Dalton, but he'd spent some of his youth in a facility where they studied the breeding of shifters and humans. He was…hurt there. It's why I get angry at Apex for you. For Kane. Callum had scars on his insides that never got better until I was almost old enough to take a pride. He wanted me to fit in with my people. He didn't have that with the gorillas, so he trained me to think like a lion, but brawl like a silverback. I had a darkness inside of me, always wanted to fight, couldn't control the animal unless I had a steady flow of good battles. He saw that, saw it would be hard for me to transition into pride life, and when I turned eighteen, he cut me loose. Put me on a small pride, two females, the male was older and had more fighting experience, but Callum didn't think I should wait until I was older. He said the darkness would get bigger without lionesses under me to keep me steady. He said that's what happened to him. He was silverback of a family group when he was taken into the facility, and after he was broken, he couldn't fit back in. He couldn't breed the females without flashbacks of what they did to him in that place, so he stayed alone, and he got worse. He didn't want that for me. He wanted me to be okay, but at eighteen, I was a hellion." Beast smiled and let off this tiny laughing sound. Now only six feet separated them. He flashed her a wicked grin. "It was good I was raised by a giant silverback who could keep me in line. The lions would've stood no chance. Before my first fight for females, Callum said he felt good about the man I turned into, and he felt better on the inside because of it. He said, 'You'll be Beast now. Someday you won't need the name anymore, and you'll call me and give it back.' I never knew what he meant by that, but I think about it a lot. I will always be Beast. My given name is unfamiliar to me. Callum found a female gorilla shifter a couple years ago. A mate. It's not supposed to work like that for the silverbacks, a single mate, but for some it does. For Callum it did. Soren didn't fit anywhere either, and now they're happy. She doesn't call him Beast. She calls him Callum."

Kiera's heart was so full by the end. She didn't know Callum, but he was probably the reason Beast turned out okay. Even though she'd never met the gorilla, a piece of her adored him for what he survived and for giving a troubled shifter a home and a future. For finding his own happiness. "What is your given name?" she asked softly.

Beast shook his head. "Doesn't matter."

It stung a little he wouldn't share that part with her, but it was unfair of her heart to demand so much so soon. He'd already shared more than she ever thought a man like him would be able to.

"I like the name Beast. It suits you. And I don't mind your scars like you think I do. If I stare, it's because I think your face is interesting."

Now only four feet separated them. Beast avoided her gaze, but he stooped and picked up another stick, handed it to her, but didn't let go of his end. They walked along like that, holding the branch between them. It was the most intimate moment she'd ever shared with another person.

"I think your face is interesting, too. And your purple hair and your nose ring and your lips—" A growl blasted from him, and he dropped his end of the stick. He placed his hands behind his back again. He tried to put another couple of feet between them but she chased him and kept their distance the same.

He cast her a quick sideways smile. It looked shy. Shy? Were his cheeks red, too? Now her cheeks felt hot. This man was something else.

Suddenly, he drew to a stop in front of her, halting her in her tracks. The grin had fallen from his lips, and he searched her face. "I didn't kill them." He ran his hand over his short hair and looked off with a confused expression. "Or maybe I did, I don't know, because I didn't do enough to save them. They were mine to protect, and I failed them instead."

Kiera's eyes stung with tears at the bone-deep loss Beast had endured. His pride had been killed, and he carried the guilt. "Is that why you let the rumors go? Is that why you never told anyone differently?"

When he looked back at her, his face was a fearsome mask, but his eyes were so clear, so blue, so full of pain. He nodded once. His nose twitched in a pissed-off lion expression. "I deserve the rumors."

Before she could change her mind, Kiera threw her arms around his waist and held on as tight as she could. Ignoring the long snarl that vibrated through his body, she rested her head on his chest and stared off into the woods until, little by little, the tension left his body, and the snarl turned to a soft, almost inaudible content sound.

He cupped the back of her head gently, as if he thought she would turn to dust and float away on the breeze. His other hand pressed softly onto her lower back, and he rested his cheek on the top of her head. "Don't cry, Kiera. I'm not pitiful either."

Was she crying? She sniffed and took stock of her body. Her cheeks stung where her tears had chilled in the cold wind, and her shoulders were shaking. Oh, she knew what he was saying. She'd told him she was strong instead of weak earlier, and he'd just done the same with her.

Something gray blurred by, snatched the stick out of her hand, and bolted away. Startled, Kiera lurched back, then laughed at the retreating dog with the giant stick hanging out of his mouth.

Beast took a quick step toward the dog, but Kiera grabbed his hand. "Let him have it, Beast. It's just a stick."

"Just a stick," he murmured with a frown in his voice.

Beast stood still like a hunting predator, his lightening eyes trained on the dog as it disappeared into the woods.

"Whose dog is that?"

"That little fucker belongs to no one. He's supposed to be Kane's, but he runs wild up here. Name's Gray Dog. Smells like a sewer rat."

Kiera snorted, and when Beast cast her a confused look, she cracked up. "That was funny."

Beast looked down between them, where their hands were still clasped. "I'm not a toucher."

"Right." She snatched her hand away and hid her disappointment by looking back toward Kane's house. "Sorry, it was just a reaction. I'm not a toucher either."

Beast's blond eyebrows drew down slightly. "Truth." His voice sounded surprised. "I thought since you were human, you would be needy, like Emma."

"Emma's a wolf," Kiera argued, turning them to the incline that led to Kane's house.

"Only recently. She needs petting all the time. Winter, too. So do Dustin and Logan and Kane and Rowan. Everybody's lost their goddamned minds up here. PDA everywhere. Can't escape it ever."

"You just hugged me back," Kiera said cheerfully, walking backward in front of him. "Did you hate that?"

Beast cracked a smile. "Yes. It was gross."

"Oh, super-gross," Kiera played along. "Bleh, hugs and affection, who wants that?"

"Not me," Beast said, but he was chuckling now. "Truthfully, I never did, though. You haven't lived in a pride, so you don't know what it's like."

"For alpha males?"

Beast nodded thoughtfully, his gaze on the woods as he followed her along slowly. "Females don't need the affection. Don't want it. They want to be taken care of during their heat cycles, and then it's back to being friends."

Nope, she didn't like the sound of him fucking his females through their heat cycles. She'd had a couple of estrus cycles before she'd been cleansed, and she'd been a hormonal little heathen, wanting to be touched three times a day until it was through. The vision of Beast screwing other girls made her hands claw up, but then she thought about what he'd really admitted. "So you're saying you've never made love to a woman?"

"No such thing."

"Oooooh Beast, if only you knew."

He narrowed his eyes to blue slits. "Have you?"

"I've had human boyfriends. Some of them do believe in making love."

"I don't like talking about this." Indeed, he was snarling pretty fiercely. The pretty blue had disappeared from his eyes and had morphed to an angry gold. Suddenly, he scented the air and asked, "What's wrong with you?"

Kiera offered him an offended sound and turned around, giving him her back. "What do you mean?"

"You smell sick."

Kiera resisted the urge to rest her hands on her

belly for comfort. "It's personal."

"Are you dying?"

She cast him a glance over her shoulder to make sure he was being serious. "No."

"Good," he rumbled, gaze on the gravel.

Maybe Logan was right, and the shifters up here really hadn't been around a pregnant woman. But…that didn't make sense for Beast. He'd been alpha of a pride for ten years. Surely, he'd been around pregnant females before. This scent should've been the most familiar one to him. Male lions obsessed over the smell of pregnancy hormones. It meant they'd been successful. She couldn't come right out and ask him, or she risked giving away the pregnancy, and she wasn't sure she was ready for that yet. This still felt like her secret to keep, at least for a little while longer until she made a decision either way.

Beast walked her all the way to Kane's door, then locked one arm against the frame and looked like he wanted to say more. He got caught up staring at her lips, though, and a part of Kiera wished he would kiss her.

He was the most handsome, intriguing man she'd

ever met. He'd been through hell, like she had, and he'd come out of it. Perhaps not whole, but he was still here fighting. Also like her. She never thought she would feel this way about a closed-off, damaged man like Beast, but he seemed like a kindred spirit.

He was all dominance, gruffness, and infinite rough edges, but he'd also just shown her a glimpse of his beautiful soul.

She stepped closer and gripped his sweater in her fists. He searched her eyes for a few moments more before he leaned down, pressed his forehead against hers, and rolled his eyes closed. A few heart pounding moments more and he eased away, then drifted down the porch steps. She'd never felt so thoroughly kissed in all her life, and he hadn't even touched his lips to hers.

"You're terrifying," he said.

Kiera smiled at him as he walked away. "Good."

Beast turned and came to a stop in the middle of Kane's yard, then linked his hands behind his head, lifting his sweater just enough to show a sexy strip of his lower abs. He canted his head and dragged his gaze up and down her body, hesitating on her curves. Her breath stuttered in her chest. With just a look, he had caressed the length of her.

"Tomorrow is Saturday." He shrugged and rolled his eyes heavenward. "We call it D-Team Sucks Saturday, and we grill out at the trailer park. If you want to come, you have the invite."

Kiera bit her bottom lip to hide how much pleasure his invitation gave her. She leaned her elbows onto the porch railing and admitted, "I had full plans to chase you out of these mountains."

Beast didn't look startled like she'd expected. Instead, his wicked smile deepened. "Same."

Kiera giggled. Fucking sexy, scar-faced lion, making her heart race with his honesty and that devilish glint in his eye. "Now you're the terrifying one."

Beast turned and strode away, his gait graceful like the massive predator that dwelled inside of him. A single word echoed through the clearing as he disappeared down the road. "Good."

SIX

Kiera practically floated into the open doorway of Kane's cabin. The dark dragon had his brown eyes narrowed on her as if she'd lost her mind, but screw everyone's opinion right now. She really, really liked Beast.

And his almost kiss? Such a delicious tease that made her want to chase him. Oh, that big brawling man knew exactly what he was doing. He was stealing her heartstrings one by one.

"You okay there?" Kane asked.

"Hmm?" Kiera asked. "Oh, yes. I'm great."

"Really? Because the other day when I saw you for the first time, you were pretty emotionally charged."

"Right." Kiera frowned and cleared her throat, strove for seriousness. If only the damn grin on her lips would quit perking up.

His blond-haired mate, Rowan, was sitting at the kitchen table with a knowing smile stretching her mouth. "We watched you on the video camera," she blurted out excitedly.

"Wait, what?"

"Roe," Kane reprimanded her.

"I'm not sorry," Rowan said with her eyes round as the moon. "I've never seen Beast be nice like that. He almost kissed you!"

"He almost kissed me!" Kiera exclaimed, excitement bubbling up in her throat as Rowan clapped and stomped her feet on the wooden floors as though she couldn't contain her giddiness.

Kiera wiggled her butt in a victory dance that now matched Rowan's as they both cracked up, and Kane's black eyebrows arched up and he looked from Kiera to Rowan, and back to Kiera. "Everyone in here has lost their damn mind but me. Reminder, Beast is half-crazed and should be managed with care."

Rowan barked a single, bellowing laugh. "Kane, you should know better than anyone that man won't be managed. Besides, I think Kiera can handle him. She's ex-lioness, current-badass. She looked like she was *managing* him just fine out there to me."

Usually, it made Kiera really defensive when someone brought up her lioness, but Rowan hadn't said it to hurt her. And really, it was kind of nice having that secret out in the open here. She wasn't pretending to be human, or lion. She was just her—Kiera the Cleansed, so okay. She wasn't going to get her feelings hurt when people mentioned it. *It is what it is*, and all.

Kane locked his arms against the table and sighed, his eyes on Kiera. "I have a question to ask you. And I know it's soon. Too soon maybe, but it feels right, and I'm gonna do it."

Kiera sat down gingerly in the chair next to Rowan. "Okay. Ask."

"I've contacted an RV rental company, and I can have one out here for you as soon as tomorrow. I can set it up in the trailer park."

"Why? I'm fine in the motel." Kiera's hackles were up. She was a roamer, and Kane was trying to get her to grow roots like a stagnant tree.

"How much money do you have left?"

"None of your business."

"Do you plan on getting a job here?"

"No."

"And when you run out of money, what will you do?"

She shrugged stubbornly. "Whatever the fuck I want to."

"Will you let me pay for an extended stay at the motel?"

Kiera huffed a breath and looked at Rowan to see if Kane was really serious.

Rowan smiled apologetically. "We really want you to stay."

Kane sat in the chair across the table from her. "At least until I have my dragon or instincts…or *whatever* convinced that you're okay."

"I'm fine."

"Then why did you come here, Kiera?" Kane asked. His eyes lightened to green, and his pupils elongated. Hello dragon. "Why did you come find me? Why did you tell me you were in trouble? Why do you smell sick? Look, I'm not asking you to stay permanently. I'm asking you to stop running for long enough to take a breather. Spend some time here, shoot the shit with people who don't care about your past, drink, eat, be fucking merry because I know you've gone through hell. Everyone could use a break sometimes, Kiera. Just...stay for a while."

Kiera crossed her arms over her chest and stared out the window at the churning gray storm clouds outside. She didn't like being pressured. She liked traveling light, little baggage, little reason to stay in a place too long. It was easiest that way. But maybe she should stay here and see what kind of life her cub would have. To see—God, she was so pathetic—to see what kind of life she could've had if she hadn't gotten so jaded getting here.

"Kiera," Kane said sternly. The dragon wasn't going to let her ignore her way out of this.

"Can I think about it?"

"Of course," Rowan said. "Whatever you need."

Kane's mouth stayed in a disapproving, thin grimace, as though he wanted an answer now, but Kiera stood before he could push the matter. She rushed to escape, but as she reached the door, Rowan called, "See you tomorrow, Kiera. Prep the liver. We drink on D-Team Sucks Saturdays."

Kiera hesitated at the door, and without turning

around, nodded once. Then she stepped out into the cold wind, shutting the door behind her, her heartbeat hammering against her sternum.

She turned and stared at the closed door. Her fingers tingled, and the baby was going crazy, rolling and kicking. Was this a sign? Kane had just offered her the world. He didn't realize it, but he had. If only she could settle… But it wouldn't work. A few more weeks here, and she would have the urge to roam again, like her frozen inner animal demanded it. Rogues did that. They migrated constantly. Lucky her, she was a human with the instincts of a lonely lioness.

She pressed her hand over her stomach to see if she could feel the kicking from the outside yet, but still couldn't. Casting a glance at the camera in the top corner of the porch roof, she bolted for her El Camino and got inside as fast as she could.

If she was different, if she was better, she could find happiness in a little RV in these beautiful mountains. That fate wasn't for her, though. The most she could hope for was that fate for her cub.

Why was she crying again?

Kiera gripped the wheel as she pulled a wide

circle in Kane's yard and rolled her tires onto the gravel road that would lead out of these mountains. Her emotions swung wide. It was the hormones, absolutely, but it was also that she'd started caring about someone above herself. Someone tiny, who depended on her to give it a good life. Someone perfect and unbroken. Someone she wanted to end up so much better than herself.

As she passed the dirt road that forked off the main, she had this overwhelming urge to go find Beast, tell him what Kane had offered, and ask his opinion on what she should do. Like he knew anything about her. Like he would have the answers.

Why did it feel like he had answers? Like he could give clarity?

Why did he feel so damn important now?

Kiera hit the gas and zoomed over the bridge and up the steep incline. These woods did something to her. They were magic or something, tempting her to dream about a future she knew in her heart would never stick.

It would be best if she took some distance to make this decision and not come back tomorrow.

SEVEN

She wasn't coming.

Beast swallowed yet another snarl as he checked the entrance to the trailer park for the hundredth time in an hour.

What was his obsession with this woman? He'd never attached to someone like this. Not ever. Not with any of his pride females, not with friends, not even with Callum. It's what had made him such a good alpha. He could manage the females, made sure none felt left out because he gave equal attention to all. He could put his head down and get shit done, but since Kiera had wandered into the territory, his mind revolved like a tornado, and the soft-spoken beauty sat right in the eye of the storm.

He was irritable and swatted Dustin's hand away when he tried to grip his shoulder. "Don't touch me."

"You can touch me," Emma said to her mate, waggling her eyebrows from where she sat in an eye-scorching purple bag chair Dustin had probably bought just to burn Beast's retinas out.

When Dustin leaned over her and started loudly sucking her neck, Beast hated everything. He checked the ribs, slathered on another layer of barbecue sauce, then closed the lid to the grill.

"Why the fuck is that ugly RV sitting here?" Beast asked grumpily. "This place was actually looking decent."

"You have a neon orange No Trespassing sign on your fence," Logan said in a judgmental voice.

Failing to see his point, Beast stopped chugging his beer and growled, "So?"

"So you might as well put some pink flamingos in the yard, too. Plus, you have a dick trophy in your window!" Logan's eyes were blazing silver. Fine with Beast, he could use a fight, and Logan's bear was a good match for his lion.

"Dude, chill," Dustin murmured. "She'll be here."

"What?" Beast wanted to clip his legs out from

under him for assuming he knew his mind. The wolf had gotten it right, but still. "I don't care about her."

Kane lifted the grill lid and said blandly, "Lie. Big lie. It wasn't even close to the truth."

"You know," Dustin said, "when I'm super grumpy, Emma gives me a hand job, and all is right with the world again."

"It's true," Emma said. "Maybe you need to get laid, Beast." Smartass was smiling like she was hilarious.

The high five Dustin gave Emma made Beast want to rip his sweater down the middle and roar until everyone stopped talking. He needed moonshine to get through tonight, not beer, but alas, Dustin had gone in and stolen his whole fucking stash and left him with only empty mason jars.

He would need to go to the shooting range again soon and blow off steam. He was going to draw Dustin's face on his target. Logan's, too.

"The RV is for Kiera," Kane said from beside Beast.

Beast stopped pulling the ribs off the grill and stared dumbfounded at the alpha. "She's staying here? In the park?" He gauged the distance between his trailer and her RV. "Just fifty yards from my den?"

"Well," Kane drawled out, "she's putting off an answer, and I don't have a good feeling since she didn't show tonight. I thought if she saw it, she would be more likely to say yes."

"Oh, she's showing," Dustin said confidently.

"How do you know?" Beast asked.

"Because I stole all her clothes, her bras, shampoo, and make-up, and left a note that said if she wants them back, she needs to make like a cow and moooove her ass on over to Kane's Mountains tonight. Told her I'd burn her shit if she stood you up." Dustin smiled brightly at Beast. "Because friends do stuff like this for each other. I'll actually burn them, too. I wasn't bluffing."

Emma snuggled up to the kleptomaniac like he was cute. Beast was totally without words. A sharp headache was forming right behind his eyes, and he pinched the bridge of his nose to relieve it.

The soft hum of an engine sounded, and everyone straightened up immediately. Everyone except Emma, who couldn't hear well in her human form and was looking around with confusion in her big green eyes.

Beast hurried to remove the rest of the food from the grill, set it on the long wooden buffet table Kane had bought for the park, bolted for the switch for the outdoor lights, flipped them on to immerse the sprawling covered gazebo in sparkling illumination, and then ran his hand over his short hair a few times…like that would do anything. Fuck, maybe he should change his shirt. He was wearing white today and had a barbecue stain on the hip. Frantically, he scrubbed at it with a napkin. He glanced up, got a flash of the D-Team staring at him, scrubbed some more, then slowed and stopped. He looked back up at the crew. They were all frozen, their eyes trained on him like he'd morphed into a four-headed octopus.

"What?" he asked, too loud. The question echoed through the trailer park.

"Did you just primp?" Logan asked.

Heat flared into his cheeks like he was a damn prepubescent teenage girl at a boy-band concert. Hell and balls. "No. Everyone shut up."

Looking totally mushy, Winter stood and meandered to him, then hugged him as if he'd invited her to do so. "You look great, Beast."

"No touching."

When Dustin made his stupid sign for how much he loved him again, Beast wanted to kick everything.

For a moment he thought he was going to have to pry the weepy little barnacle off of him, but thankfully Winter unhanded him before Kiera drove under the Blackwing Mobile Park sign. Friggin' D-Team.

He cast the RV one more look and quickly tried to process his feelings about her living so close. He waited for the lion to revolt, but the snarly horn-ball thought it was a great idea. *Pussy every night*, his inner lion cheered. Fantastic. He should put himself into a cage now.

Beast gave his attention to Kiera's headlights and picked up the present he'd gotten her. As he walked by, Dustin tried to hug him like Winter had, but Beast swatted his hands away. "Don't ruin this," he snarled at the D-Team, cast them a last fiery glare, then strode to meet Kiera.

Down to his bones, Beast knew there was a 100% chance those idiots would absolutely chase her away.

****

Kiera inhaled sharply at the scar-faced giant headed her way with those long, confident strides of his. Her fury with the thieving wolf evaporated into thin air.

Beast knew his exact place in the world, and that was at the very tippy-top of the food chain. Every time she saw him, he caused a stronger chemical reaction between her legs than he had the time before.

This time was no different. Kiera squeaked and clamped her legs closed.

His face was serious, his mouth set in a grim line, eyes blazing gold. He was a beautiful hellion come to earth. His wide shoulders pushed perfectly against a white cotton long-sleeved shirt. Holy heaven, the man could wear white.

Kiera pulled to a stop on the side of the dirt road and cut the engine and headlights.

She got out and opened her mouth to explain she was just here to get her stuff that Dustin stole, but Beast held his hand stiffly out for a shake. "I want to hug you, but those fuck-faces won't let me live it down, so…" Beast's lip twitched up in a snarl, then lowered again.

Baffled, Kiera slid her palm against his and shook it. He canted his head, and his nostrils flared as he sniffed. "Have you been crying?"

"No," she lied.

He arched one blond brow up high. "Bullshit. Who made you cry?"

She let off a soft laugh because he was still shaking her hand. "Kane, actually."

Beast looked furious in the moment before he glanced back over his shoulder at the Blackwing Crew gathered around a long table and filling plates with food. The Blackwings were pretending not to pay attention, but every one of them were casting her and Beast sideways glances.

"Do you want me to challenge him?" Beast asked.

Kiera blinked slowly. "You want to challenge the End of Days?"

Beast's fair brows lowered to a scowl as he gave his attention back to her. "I didn't say I'd survive it."

Kiera tried not to laugh, really she did, but he was so earnest in his question to avenge her tears. So ready to brawl.

Beast yanked his hand away from hers. "You're laughing at me."

Kiera lurched forward and hugged his waist. It was like embracing a stone statue. "Kane didn't do anything mean. He just gave me stuff to think about. Hard stuff. I cry too easily right now."

Dustin let off an ear-piercing cat-call whistle from near the pretty, lit-up gazebo.

Beast sighed a defeated sound and wrapped his arms gently around her shoulders. "You cry easy because you're sick? Or because you are human?"

"Both, kind-of."

"I made you meat."

Kiera bit back her smile. "What kind of meat?"

His heart was hammering so hard against her cheek. "Ribs. And baked potatoes. And orange slices and salad because Dustin gave me this stupid list of what human women like and apparently you like to watch your figures."

"I'm not watching my figure." Baby wouldn't allow it.

Beast heaved a sigh. "Good, because watching you eat rabbit-food would be gross."

A laugh bubbled up her throat, and suddenly she felt better than she had...well...since the last time she'd seen him. Beast had this uncanny ability to make her forget her problems.

Beast sniffed the top of her head. "I like your purple hair. You smell like tears and vanilla, and I like vanilla. And you look really nice in your baggy sweater."

She had eased back so she could watch his face while he gave her weird compliments. He was looking up at the star-speckled sky.

"Was that on the human list?" she asked.

"Yeah, Dustin said complimenting is good. And also presents." Beast handed her a stick.

Kiera took it gently. The shape was familiar, but she was completely baffled why he would give her a branch with a red bow on it.

"I looked everywhere for it. That's the one Gray Dog stole from you." Beast inhaled deeply and shrugged. "And now that I'm thinking about it, a stick is a really dumb present."

Stunned, Kiera looked at the stick against her palms. It was the one she and Beast had held together. He'd tracked it down? For her? This might be the sweetest thing a man had ever done. "No, Beast. This is a really good present. I'll keep it always."

"Yeah?"

Throat tight, she nodded.

"Good. Don't tell Dustin I read the list, though. He'll be an obnoxious asshole for the rest of my life about it." Beast cleared his throat and shifted his weight side-to-side. "I'm…you know…glad you like it."

"I *really* like it. And the ribs smell really good," she murmured, completely smitten and amused by this man who could walk like he owned the earth but who stumbled over his words around her.

Beast ran his hand up the back of his head and gave her a self-deprecating smile. "This is the first time I've cooked for the crew. I wanted to be the one to feed you tonight." He swallowed hard and shook his head, and now he wouldn't meet her eyes.

Kiera squared up to him again and cupped his face. His whiskers tingled against her palms. "It's just me, Beast."

He pressed his palms over her hands to keep her touch on his face. In a whisper, he said, "That doesn't help."

"Why not?"

"Because you feel like everything. My chest feels so tight, and I'm fucking everything up because I'm not good at words like Logan or Kane or Dustin, and I can't stop thinking about you still. Or talking apparently."

Kiera pushed up on her tiptoes and hugged his neck, pressed her body along his. Against his ear, she said, "I like you just like this."

Beast slid his hands up her back, gently squeezing up her spine every few inches as if kneading her like a cat. It felt so good she rolled her eyes closed against the stars and relaxed against him.

"I like that you have curves, too," he murmured. "You aren't skin and muscle like other lionesses. I like it when you hug me. The big sweaters hide you from the others, but you let me touch you."

She huffed a soft breath. He didn't know what they were, but he didn't mind her baby curves. Something about that loosened her heart up even more. Her pants didn't fit, and she'd grown fuller in all areas of her body, but here was this perfect specimen of a man telling her he still thought she was pretty.

"Food's getting cold!" Logan barked.

The sound of a smack echoed through the clearing.

"Ow, what was that for?" Logan asked loud enough for even Kiera to hear. She thought it had been his mate, Winter, who had smacked him, but Dustin was the one that reprimanded him. "Stop being a cock-blocker, you dunce."

"They aren't doing anything but hugging a lot," Logan argued.

"I think I hate them," Beast muttered.

Kiera snorted and then settled the stick in the passenger's seat so she wouldn't lose it. Over her shoulder, she said, "I want some of that food before it's all gone."

Beast cleared his throat again when she busted him for staring at her butt as she crawled back out of her car. "You go on." He backed up a few steps into the shadows.

"What? No, I want to go with you. Why are you going that way?"

"Because I'm hard as a friggin' rock right now, and I'm not going over there full-mast, Kiera."

Her mouth plopped open, but when she looked at the zipper of his jeans, yep, boner-city. And it was the biggest city on boner continent. She tried not to stare, really she did, but hell yes.

Beast covered his crotch with his giant hands. "You aren't helping if you look at it all hungry like that."

"Well, think about something gross. I don't want to go over there without you."

"Fuck, fuck, fuck," Beast gritted out. He closed his eyes and blew out a deep breath.

"What are you thinking about?" She couldn't help the question, the curious kitty in her had to know.

"Dustin hugging me. Salad. Dustin stealing from me. Salad dressing. Dustin's stupid face. Okay, I'm good, let's go." He strode past her and grabbed her hand on the way.

She yelped as she pushed her legs to keep up with his long strides. "What else was on the human list?" she asked.

"Uuuh, girls like when you pick their wedgies when their nails are wet, and they don't like when you go too long without manscaping. They like flowers, the plants or the seeds. Also, when you go on your period, I should buy you chocolate and watch sappy movies with you. Don't make fun of you when you cry, and you'll yell at me less."

Kiera was pursing her lips hard to stifle her

laughter. Beast sounded so serious right now.

"Do you want to see my den?" he asked suddenly.

"Yes."

"Well, you can't right now because it's off in the trees." He pointed. "And Dustin said your vision probably sucks."

"Uh, my vision doesn't suck that bad, but..." She squinted into the shadows, but all she could make out was the dark outline of a building. "Yeah I can't see that from here." She could, however, see a shiny silver RV parked near the gazebo. "Uuuuh, what is that?" she asked, fury rocketing through her blood, because oh, she knew.

"Your den."

"It's not my den because I haven't said yes to staying here."

Beast cast her a sharp look, then pulled her into the ring of light that surrounded the gazebo. He pointed to her. "This is Kiera."

"Uh, we know, Romeo," Dustin said from his seat closest to them.

Beast released her hand and lurched at Dustin. The wolf winced and jerked away from the railing as a soft whine wrenched from his throat. Beast's smile was positively devilish, and though Kiera desperately wanted to hold onto her anger at Kane for renting the damn RV and putting more pressure on her, another accidental grin graced her lips. God, she had the biggest crush on him. He was a total rough-and-tumble, brawler caveman, but she was finding she really, *really* liked that about him.

Kiera gave a little wave to the Blackwing Crew, who were eating around a giant table on the gazebo. "Good to see you all again. Except for you Kane." Kiera pointed to the RV and arched her eyebrow.

Kane shrugged and gulped down a bite. "Never said I played fair, Kiera. You want a tour of it? We rented you the deluxe suite."

"Polite decline. I'm fine at the motel."

"Fine to run away whenever the wind switches directions," Dustin muttered.

"I want my stuff back," she gritted out to the wolf.

"You have stripper clothes. Are you a stripper?"

"Why did you go through my things?"

Dustin looked offended that she'd ask such a silly question. "Because it's fun. If you are a stripper, can you teach Emma how to dance on one of those poles? I can get one installed in our trailer."

"Not a stripper, Dustin. I'm a cocktail waitress."

"She said cock," Emma said proudly.

When Beast sighed a tired sound, Kiera hid her smile by giving her attention to filling her plate. Those two didn't need any encouragement.

"So you really don't know how to pole dance?" Dustin sounded so disappointed.

"I can remember a fifteen drink order like it's nothing, but nope. No pole training for me." Kiera plopped a rack of ribs onto her plate and dished out some salad because she actually did like the stuff. "I did dance in one of those clear cages once at this fancy bar called Barky's in a ritzy part of Chicago. I lived with three roommates at the time. We all worked there, and we had to ride the L every night to get there."

"What's the L?" Winter asked. She was leaning over the table with her cheek on her fist, attention riveted on Kiera like it was story time.

"It's an elevated train that travels through the city. It was fun. That was the longest I stayed in one place. I liked my roommates."

"And you liked dancing in clear cages," Dustin said.

"I only did that on Thursday nights. The other nights I served drinks, and when I did dance, I was fully clothed."

"Why did you move?" Kane asked.

"Uuuh…" How did she explain Justin? "Boy problem, and then the city didn't feel as safe anymore. I just moved away from there a couple months ago. Been bouncing around a bit since, trying to figure out what to do next."

"Perfect timing," Kane said. "We have an RV with your name on it. Literally. Dustin, for whatever fucking reason, wrote your name in purple crayon on the wall like a toddler."

"Bitches love purple."

Kane slapped him upside the head so hard Dustin coughed out a piece of food.

Beast strode up the stairs in a blur and dropped his plate on the table. "I dare you to say *bitch* again."

"Okay, clearly this is a cultural misunderstanding," Dustin said, raising his hands in surrender. "I'm a wolf, and female dogs are called bitches. Don't eat me."

Kiera made her way to Beast and rested her hand on his back. To Dustin, she asked, "How are you still alive?"

"That's still a mystery to most of us," Rowan said around a bite of baked potato.

"These guys wouldn't really kill me. They like to threaten, choke, and bite me, but at the end of the day, they love me."

"I don't," Beast muttered, sitting down in an empty chair.

Logan raised his hand like he was in school. "Also don't love you."

"I tolerate you," Kane said.

"You're growing on me," Winter said cheerfully. "I only want to claw you fifty percent of the time now."

"I love you," Emma said, clamping her teeth gently onto the werewolf's shoulder.

Dustin ran his hand through his shoulder length hair, draped his arm around the back of his mate's chair, and grinned like he'd shown them all. "See?"

Beast offered Kiera a dead-eyed look and a tired shake of his head before he shoved the seat next to him out from under the table for her.

"Thanks," Kiera said breathlessly, flattered at his sweet gesture.

When she sat down, Beast dragged her chair closer to him. One fiery warning glance at Logan, who sat on her other side, and then Beast dug into his dinner.

Rowan was smiling big at her and Beast with giant, happy blue eyes. Emma and Dustin were now making out. Logan was snarling to himself as he ate, while Winter nuzzled her face against her mate's arm like he wasn't a growly psycho-person. Kane was staring at Kiera as if he expected her to bolt, and Beast was glaring at the salad on her plate with a suspicious grimace, like she might as well be eating bugs.

Kiera giggled. She couldn't help it. These people were just as crazy as she'd assumed them to be when she'd been stalking them. But...she kind of liked them. Beast especially.

As the conversation ebbed and flowed, Beast relaxed beside her, and twice, he even brushed her leg with his and cast her a quick smile that gave her an immediate warm sensation between her thighs. For a man who didn't like touch, he was warming up slowly to her. And for as little as she had needed touch in her own life, she got the biggest butterfly flutters in her stomach when Beast gave her even the slightest affection.

He liked her. She could tell by the things he did. He offered to refill her plate when she finished and immediately defended her choice of bottled water when Dustin tried to pressure her into taking a shot of tequila. He leaned back in his chair and fiddled with her hair almost absently while he listened to Dustin drone on about how he was going to make an obstacle course along the edge of the trailer park so he could prove he was some sort of ultimate ninja-shifter. She caught Beast watching her a couple dozen times, but he always looked away quick. And when everyone was clearing their plates to end the night, he stayed in his seat and gently rested his palm on her thigh as though she was fragile.

"Don't go yet," he said low. "I'm not ready."

That admission drew another smile from her lips, and she scooted her chair closer to his.

"Cold?" he asked with a slight frown.

"A little. Dustin stole my jacket."

"Dustin, put her stuff in her car," Beast barked

out.

"Fine, but I'm keeping the sparkly booty shorts for Emma," Dustin said over his shoulder as he walked his mate across the dirt road toward a doublewide trailer.

Fine with Kiera, she didn't fit into them anymore.

She curled up her legging-clad knees under her baggy sweater and faced Beast, then wrapped her arms around herself to stay warm.

"I never wished I was like Dustin before," he said, shredding a napkin on the table. When he cast her a quick glance, his frown was deep. "But tonight I kind of did."

"Why?"

"Emma used to be human. Recently, actually. He's good at touching her. She smiles when he does it right. I can tell she feels safe with him. You still smell nervous, maybe even a little scared sometimes."

"That's not because of you. That's because of stuff going on in my head."

"What stuff?"

"Leaving." She fiddled with a loose thread on the hem of her sweater and shrugged. "Staying. It's scary either way."

Beast inhaled deeply. "I understand that. I haven't registered to the crew yet. I have the paperwork all filled out, but I can't bring myself to take them to the courthouse. Kane's getting upset. Demoting me. Relying on Logan more. He'll boot me out of the running for Third in the crew soon."

"Do you want Third?"

He huffed a humorless sound. "I was alpha of a big pride for a decade, Kiera. What do you think?"

"That you wouldn't do well at the bottom of a crew."

He shook his head slowly.

"Well," she murmured, hugging his big bicep and resting her cheek against his strength. "Why don't you go to the courthouse and secure your spot under the dragons?"

He swallowed audibly and relaxed under her embrace. He leaned closer and rubbed his whiskered cheek against the top of her head. She smiled because her mother used to do that. It was a quick sign of affection for lions. She wondered if Beast even realized he'd done it.

"I'm scared of getting close to them."

"To the D-Team?"

He gave a single nod.

"Because you lost your pride?" she asked, her throat tightening over the words.

"I thought I would be safe in this crew. I thought they wouldn't touch me, wouldn't make me feel. It wasn't a pride, no lions, so I thought I would just hide out here in Kane's Mountains for the rest of my days. Wait to die, you know?"

"Yeah." She hugged him tighter. "I know that feeling."

"It was a bachelor group that did it. Not me." Beast wouldn't meet her gaze, but she could see the gold color from here. "It was twelve on one. They wanted the pride. These bachelors, though…" Beast gritted his teeth. "They would destroy it from the inside out, and my females fought back, fought beside me. I wanted them to run, so they could live, but they wouldn't leave me. They died trying to keep me king."

"Oh, my gosh," she whispered. "But…why? Bachelor groups aren't allowed to make moves like that."

"They felt justified."

"Why?" she asked, sitting up straight.

Beast angled his head toward her, and his eyes

were ancient as he murmured, "Because I didn't make cubs. Couldn't do it. Tried for a decade." He ran his hands down his scruff and sighed as he stared at the dark woods beyond the trailer park. "And I wanted them so fucking bad, Kiera. Wanted to raise them good, like Callum raised me. I wanted to give my females the families they wanted. I wanted to make them happy." He eased out of her grip, slid his hands over his short hair, and stayed like that, head angled down, hiding his face from her. "Do you know about the council?"

The lion council? Yes, they were ruthless assholes who had their hand in all affairs to do with lion shifters. Nosy, dominant males who liked to make up rules. They'd been relentless in pressuring her mom to pick a pride. "Yes," she whispered. "I know them."

"Well, they started putting pressure on me to have cubs, like I wasn't trying hard enough, and I could see it. There was unrest with our people because I had this huge pride, but no offspring. Other males thought they could do better. I treated my females well, though, and nobody asked them if they wanted a power-shift. We were all still trying. I didn't know, but there was a coup going on behind my back. I should've seen it coming. I couldn't do the one fucking thing I was supposed to do and couldn't hold the pride forever. It happened in the night. I tried to save them, but it was a fucking massacre, and I was left for dead. God, I wanted to die. I was lying there with them." Beast buried his face deeper into his arms, cradled the back of his head. "I couldn't move, I was so bad off, just…waiting to go, listening to silence. No heartbeats, no breathing." His shoulders jerked once like he'd been hit in the stomach, and a long, heartbroken snarl purged from his body.

Kiera rubbed his back in circles and forced her crying to stay silent because this was his moment, not hers. "What happened to the bachelors?"

He inhaled sharply. "Four got away. I hunted them as soon as I was recovered enough. I killed three. I'm still hunting the fourth. He's the one who started the rumors, and the council backed him up. They spread them through our people, and I just…let it happen. No one wanted to be around a rumored murderer after that, and I'd shut down from people completely, so win-win. They left me alone, and I left them alone. I waited for the council to kill me, but they never came. Even when I killed the three bachelors. I thought avenging my pride would fix me. I *prayed* vengeance would fix me." *But it didn't.* He didn't have to say that last part. It was there in the emotion in his voice. "Logan came here to have Kane put him down." Beast rolled his face toward her, and he looked so tired. "I came for the same reason. As soon as I finish the fourth bachelor, I plan to ask Kane for an honorable death."

"Beast," she whispered, her face crumpling. She'd been in a bad spot when her lion had been taken from her, but never had she wanted her life to end.

"If I can just keep separate from the D-Team, I can go through with it, but they keep making me feel shit. They keep trying to open me up, and it fucking hurts. I got so good at not feeling, and now I watch them, happy with each other, always trying to include me, touching me, making me want connections I have no business wanting. With every day that passes, I hurt more, but my survival instinct is growing. I don't know why. But I know my window to have Kane put me down is closing, and sometimes I get scared I'm going to be stuck in this hell forever. Alone."

Those words sang to her heart. *Alone.* She knew

all about that—being stuck between the shifter world and the human one.

"What a pair we make," she said thickly, hugging his bicep again and following his gaze into the dark woods.

He let off a soft, single laugh. "Yeah. Pair of misfits."

She smiled and nuzzled his strong arm. Being a misfit didn't seem so bad when he was lumping them together. Mmm, Beast smelled good. Familiar already. "Do you want to show me the RV?"

He jerked a frown at her. "Really?"

"Yeah, but swear not to tell Kane. Tricky asshole dragon doesn't need to be thinking my decisions are based on him."

"What are they based on?"

"Tonight?"

Beast nodded once, hope pooling in his gold eyes.

Kiera offered him a slow smile and whispered, "You."

EIGHT

She should tell him about the pregnancy. It didn't feel right that he'd told her so much, and she had this huge secret. He couldn't father cubs? Kiera was heartbroken for him. She couldn't imagine what that did to an alpha lion like Beast. In lion culture, everything depended on the next generation. The prides revolved around the cubs.

And here she was carrying one she hadn't even tried for. It was this huge white elephant in the room that Beast was unaware of and cast a wave of consuming guilt over Kiera's shoulders.

But tonight had been perfect, and she didn't know Beast well enough to guess his reaction. What if he bolted? What if he didn't want another lion's offspring in the territory and chased her away? Shit. Maybe she should've been more upfront with all of this in the first place, but she'd wanted to make sure this was an option she wanted to explore before she told anyone about the baby. Until she trusted them fully, she couldn't risk her whereabouts getting back to Justin. He would bring hell to earth to get his cub back. Not because he had good paternal instincts. Quite the opposite, in fact. The second Justin had scented she was with child, he'd promised he would separate her from the baby and give it to one of the lionesses in his own pride to raise if she didn't pledge fealty to him. He was an awful father, completely absent other than the thirty seconds he spent making the cubs.

She'd just wanted a claiming mark from him to fix her broken lion, but everything had gone sideways.

Kiera followed behind Beast to the silver, metal Airstream trailer, while subtly cradling her belly. She wanted so much better for this baby. For *her* baby. Maybe she wanted these mountains.

Beast pulled open the door and stood to the side, his expression unreadable. Kiera smiled timidly and stepped past him up the two creaking stairs and into the little home on wheels.

There was a light switch that actually worked when she flipped it on.

"Kane must've parked it near the gazebo so he could run electricity to it for you," Beast murmured.

"Oh. Smart." And convenient. She hadn't expected it to have electricity.

Kane hadn't been lying when he'd said he got the deluxe suite. It had polished wooden floors, and the interior walls were the same polished silver that matched the exterior. On one end of the home, there was a sitting area and table. A counter and small kitchen ran along the opposite wall, miniature fridge, sink, and four-burner stove included. A small flat screen television was mounted on the wall, and on the opposite end, a comfortable looking bed took up almost a third of the living space. The wooden cabinets, floors, and table in the home were a glossed rich walnut color, and the appliances were stainless steel, like the walls. It was rustic meets modern. It was perfect.

"I like that smile," Beast said low from where he'd perched in the open doorway. "You don't smile much, but when you do, it's beautiful."

She loved his compliment, but it also made her a little sad. It was the first time anyone had pointed out how little she smiled, and funny enough, she'd noticed how much her face had transformed into a grin since she'd come here. Her cheeks were sore. Beast would really think she was pitiful if he'd known her before she came to the Smokies.

She ripped her gaze away from him so he wouldn't see how stung she felt at that realization. She made her way through the RV, opening cupboards, trying out the television, running her fingertips along the edge of the plush comforter on the bed. She didn't mind small spaces. In fact, she preferred them.

"I don't really feel safe when I sleep," she admitted, giving him something in place of the pregnancy announcement. That she wasn't ready for, but she could gift him this.

The trailer rocked as Beast climbed inside and let the door swing shut behind him. He settled onto the seat cushions by the table and asked, "Why not?"

"Since my lioness got taken, I feel different."

"Different how?"

"It's hard to explain," she drew out. Kiera sank onto the mattress and pulled her legs in crisscross-applesauce, like one of her elementary teachers had called it. "It's like I constantly feel like I'm forgetting something. Does that make sense?"

"Is it your lioness you feel like you're forgetting? Because you can't feel her anymore?"

"Yeah. So I wake up all the time, and my senses are always on alert. It's like I can't settle down enough to let my body go into a deep sleep. I move around during the night a lot, just doing dumb shit. Checking window locks or investigating every little sound. I feel like something's going to happen to me all the time." She shook her head helplessly. "I'm tired, Beast."

"Do you sleep in big rooms?" he asked, leaning onto the table. His blond brows were lowered in a worried expression that she wanted to smooth from his face. "I can't sleep in big rooms. If your lioness was dominant, and she's still in there somewhere, she won't like big spaces. You need a smaller den."

"She's not in there. She died."

"Kiera—"

"No, it's okay, Beast. I accepted it a long time ago.

I had a flare up recently when Kane got his dragon back. I thought I could get my animal back, too, but our story isn't the same. Our cleansing procedures weren't the same. I don't feel my animal at all. If I didn't hear and see better-than-average, and if I didn't have these eyes"—she gestured to the frozen lion eyes in her face—"I would think I dreamed her. I don't even remember what it feels like to share my body with the animal anymore." She shrugged and tried to smile. "Maybe that's a good thing because now I just want to move on."

"By roaming?"

"Maybe." It was a bullshit answer. She was shutting him down because she always got defensive when she felt someone digging too deep. She didn't like the way Beast leaned back in the chair, and his eyes closed down on her, too. That was her fault. "Sorry. I'm not used to answering this many questions in such a short amount of time."

Beast nodded slowly, a faraway look in his eyes as he stared at a miniature salt and pepper shaker in the middle of the table. "Kiera?"

"Hmm?"

"You have all your shit here, thanks to Dustin.

You have no reason to go back to the motel tonight. Why don't you stay here, just for the night, and actually open up to the possibility that you don't have to run forever?"

"Who says I'm running?"

"Me. That restlessness you're feeling? That's what happens to rogues who don't settle in a pride. You need to stop somewhere, just to see if you even can. Your momma was a rogue, but that don't mean you have to be one, too."

"I'm not a rogue, Beast. I'm a human."

"Bullshit," he said, making his way to the door. "You say you don't feel your lioness, but she's there. Somewhere. I can smell her, Kiera." His lip twitched slightly, and his voice lowered to a husky, gravelly tone. "I can *feel* her. She was calling to my animal before you even knew I was stalking you. I feel like a rutting alpha again being around you. No human can pull that kind of a response from a lion. Just because you can't call on her for a Change doesn't mean she's dead." Beast pulled open the door and made his way outside, and right before the door swung closed, he said, "Apex failed."

Kiera hissed. She didn't know what possessed

her to do that. She hadn't done that since she was a kid, but Beast was wrong, and he was pissing her off. He was giving her hope in words, but he had no right to. He didn't know. He didn't feel the bleak emptiness inside of her. He didn't feel the bottomless hole that once upon a time she'd tried to fill with things like drinking and partying and hell, even sleeping around. She was just getting ahold of this, just accepting it. Kiera just needed to accept being human so she could be happy with her life someday.

And here Beast was telling her he *smelled* her lioness. That he *felt* her, like she wasn't some ghost long-dead.

Well, fuck him.

Eyes burning, she blasted off the bed and stomped outside.

Beast had his back to her as he walked purposefully toward his trailer. He had to have heard her coming, but he didn't duck out of the way when she shoved him in the back.

"You have no right."

Beast snarled and rounded on her.

"You have no right to give me hope, no right to say she's still here. You aren't me! You don't feel what

I do!"

"And what is that, Kiera?"

"Nothing! I feel nothing! I'm empty."

Beast pulled her against him so fast, she didn't know what to do with all of these roiling emotions inside of her. She felt so much. Safe, angry, warm, overwhelmed. With a long sob, she sagged against him, and then before he could trap her completely in the hug, she pushed off him and made a bee-line for her car on the other side of the park.

"Where are you going?" Beast asked from right behind her.

"Home."

"And where's that, Kiera?" he barked.

"Anywhere but here! You think it would be good for me to stay in this trailer park where I'll have to watch you all shift into your precious animals while my heart gets ripped out every time? Hell no. This place would torture me. And you spouting off about my lioness like you know her—"

"I do know her."

"I don't even know her anymore! You can't know her better than me, you dick weevil douche nugget armpit shitstain... *fuck*! I don't even know what I'm saying right now I'm so angry. Stop following me."

Beast was grinning, and she wanted to claw his face off, but she didn't have fucking claws anymore, so she bent down and ripped two handfuls of wild grass from the ground and threw it at his face. It floated down in a pitiful green rain that missed him by a foot. Fuck everything. She kicked at a weed and let off a pathetic human growl when Beast got too close. If that noise didn't prove she was human, well then Beast was just as crazy as the other psychopaths in this trailer park.

"Damn, Beast," Dustin crowed from his front porch. "Kiera looks pissed! You want me to protect you from her?"

"Fuck you, *Stupid Dustin!*" Kiera said, flipping him the bird.

Beast's grin grew bigger.

"I said stop following me!" she barked at Beast. Her body was humming with something, fury perhaps. She hadn't been this mad in…ever.

Beast was taunting her, and Dustin was butting in now, too. "Sorry, no fucking me, Kiera. Emma's got that chore tonight. By the way, Stupid Dustin is a terrible insult. My IQ is kind of high. I made all As in school. And I'm a fast talker, so you know I'm smart. Do you want to try again? You could call me Douche Canoe Dustin. Dung Beetle Dustin. Dick Flake Dustin?"

Feeling insane with her anger, she flapped her hands around in front of her and stomped the next two steps. "Aaaah!"

Dustin zipped his lips and pretended to throw away the key, but he was still smiling. Stupid Dustin.

Beast felt heavy—too heavy—from behind her. That, and he was growling now, a low threatening sound that raised the hairs on the back of her neck. She swatted at it. He wouldn't hurt her, probably, but just in case, she picked up her pace.

"Bad idea running from a predator," Dustin called unhelpfully.

"I fucking know! I used to be one!" She pulled on the door handle of her El Camino, but Beast slammed the door closed again and yanked her around to face him. And his face. Was. Terrifying.

Blazing gold had taken his eyes, and when he curled his lips back, his teeth had grown sharper. Body rigid, his muscles pressed against his clothes. He was in hunter mode.

Beast cupped her neck and dipped his fiery gaze to her lips. It struck her in the seconds before he leaned into her. He wasn't hunting her. She'd riled him up. Beast pressed her against the car with his body weight and kissed her hard. So hard she tasted blood. So hard she felt his teeth. So hard she could feel every stony muscle of his torso against hers like a second skin.

Trapped! He'd trapped her against the car, was holding the back of her neck, and she was stuck in this rough kiss with a man she was so...so...

Beast released her neck and stroked his hands down her arms to her hands where he intertwined their fingers. The growl in his throat was nothing short of feral and rattled constantly, but his kiss had gone from bitey to sexy in an instant. He angled his face, pushed his tongue past her lips and into her mouth, and *oh my God*. She was supposed to be doing something right now... Raging? Running? He'd kissed her into dumbness. Every remaining working brain cell was focused on how soft his lips had suddenly turned, and the little hussies were cheering like this was the best thing that could've ever happened to her. Her traitor body rolled against him. Her traitor hands slipped under the hem of his sweater to touch his bottom two abs.

"Let me show her to you," he murmured against her lips.

What? Show what to who? His words didn't make sense, but he could've said "Let's go run naked in the snow right now," and she would've done it as long as he kept kissing her like this. Like he was breathing life into her.

When he ran her hands up his washboard stomach, a shiver trembled up his body. He gritted his teeth and rested his forehead on hers for a moment before he kissed her again. Right, he didn't like touch, but at the moment, she couldn't help herself. Beast was perfect. Dominant, manly, muscular, and could kiss like he would be a demon in the sack. And it's not like he was pulling dominant male lion shit and turning her around to fuck her from behind. He was still holding her hands and kissing her like he meant it.

Something deep inside of her was opening up. It wasn't uncomfortable, just there, at the edge of her senses. Her insides were slowly sparking with warmth and a tingling sensation. Whatever he was doing to her body, she loved it.

She moved her hands to his chest and moaned when his kisses drifted to her neck. He was a biter, but not too hard. Not too painful. It was as if he was letting her know he *could* sink his teeth into her but was in control of himself. He pulled the loose neck of her sweater aside and kissed down her collar bone to her claiming mark. When his lips brushed the first scar, he reared back and glared at it for a moment, but if he was angry, he put that emotion into kissing her again. Beast pulled her wrists down his stomach until her hands rested just at his belt-line.

Carefully, Beast slipped his hand down the front of her leggings and cupped her sex gently, dragging a sigh of ecstasy from Kiera. When he pushed a finger inside her, his body started shaking. No, it was humming with power.

He sucked hard on her bottom lip and murmured, "Woods or bed?"

"Bed," she said on a breath.

He yanked her up, and she wrapped her legs around him as he strode for his trailer. He carried her as if she weighed nothing, but perhaps to a big, powerful man like Beast, she didn't. His gait stayed smooth and long while he held her up with only one arm. His other hand was tangled in the back of her hair, pulling her close as he kissed her. For a moment, she thought he might need to see where he was going, but when she tried to pull away, he wouldn't have it. Perhaps Beast knew his territory like the back of his hand.

His body jerked as he shoved a gate open. Then they were on a porch and going through a door, and she closed her eyes to everything because she was sure he would turn on the lights, and it would be too bright.

He didn't, though. Beast stepped into his bedroom. It was completely dark except for the blue moonlight that streamed through the blinds of the window, striping her like a tiger.

Beast set her down, but stayed on her, pressing her back against a wall. He only put inches between them when he eased back to pull his shirt over his head. God, he was beautiful. Scarred all to hell, muscles rippling, tattoos covering half his body, short hair mussed from taking off his shirt, eyes glowing like an animal's in the dim lighting. He didn't give her time to study his perfectly defined chest, his sculpted eight pack, the ink that decorated his body, or the spider web of claw marks. He was back on her like he couldn't stop touching her, his lips urgent against hers.

He was going to figure this out really quick. Kiera wasn't showing a lot. She'd been in shape before getting pregnant, and her tight abs had kept her bump from popping yet, but she definitely looked like she'd eaten a big meal. Big enough to make her stomach tight as a drum and slightly rounded. But when Beast pulled her sweater over her head, his focus wasn't on her stomach. It was on her red lacy bra. Her boobs were tender and spilling out of it, and a wave of insecurity washed through her.

Beast's slow, feral smile put her at ease immediately. He lifted his gaze back to hers and unsnapped the back like he'd done it a thousand times. Perhaps he had. He ripped her bra from her and tossed it to the ground behind him. She had already kicked out of her boots, but Beast shocked her to stillness when he slid down to his knees and dragged her leggings down with him. He cast her a wicked big-cat smile that was all male bravado and utter confidence. Sexy Beast. He slid one arm behind her lower back and lifted up on his knees enough to bite her hip, kiss it, bite her hipbone, kiss it. He was working his way to her inner thighs, and Kiera was already panting in desperation, her nails on his scalp, gripping his hair, as she rolled her hips with every nip. When his lips brushed her sex, she gasped his name and rolled her eyes closed. This was everything. The care he took to make her feel good. The time he took. The slow pace he set with his tongue. Her entire body was shaking, and the pressure built and built until her legs wouldn't hold her. But Beast was there, supporting her, holding her upright. With a growl, he lifted her and settled her onto his bed. Pushing her legs open wider, he sucked on her clit, then pushed his tongue into her again, but she was already so close.

"I'm coming," she murmured mindlessly. "Beast, Beast, Beast, I'm coming."

Orgasm pulsed through her so hard her body twitched. Kiera gripped his hair, and he snarled a sexy sound as he eased back and crawled up her body. His massive arms flexed as he locked them on either side of her shoulders. Kiera was floating. She was smoke. All she could do was look up at him helplessly as her release pulsed on and on, leaving her in a haze of pleasure she couldn't escape. There was the tinkle of a belt, the rip of a zipper, and Kiera smiled drunkenly because it wasn't over. He wasn't finished with her, and a big part of her was just so happy that this moment could drag on.

Beast lifted her hand to his lips, then kissed her wrist. He kissed down to the inside of her elbow, then dragged her hand up his stomach like she'd done earlier, like he wanted that kind of touch now. Like he craved it. He was so warm, so perfect. She traced a few of the scars, but her attention drifted to his abs and to the shadows that his V of muscle made right at the top of the pants he was pushing down.

She'd never been this excited to see a man's body before.

Beast's pants hit the floor, and Kiera inhaled sharply when his thick erection jutted between them. Big, badass, alpha male Beast had known what he was doing. He'd needed to open her up, and loosen her up before he pushed inside her.

Beast went down to his elbows and pulled her hand to his ribs, then urged her palm to his back. When he dipped into her shallowly, Kiera moaned and clawed up her hand on reflex. Beast gave a look that was half sexy grimace, half wicked grin.

"Do that when I make you come again, Kiera. Let me know you like it."

Holy fuck, what? He wanted her to claw him? Ooooh. Beast thrust into her deeper, his abs flexing against her belly, and now his lips were on hers again. She could taste herself on him, but there was something erotic about sharing that. She moved her other hand to his back to feel his graceful movement when he slid into her again. Deeper this time, and she had to remind herself to relax so she could take him.

He was doing something to her, something she didn't understand. He was drawing that sensation up again, that tingling feeling that took over her body and made her feel like she was sparkling from the inside out. His fingers dug into her hip as he pushed into her again and again, all the way inside of her now, and there was so much pleasure building where he touched her she was overwhelmed by it. Her body felt so strange, so full. The hollowness was gone, and in its place was this warm hopefulness.

Beast was bucking into her faster now, and she was close, crying out every time he hit her clit, desperately gripping his hair, then clawing her fingers against the strong planes of his back, gripping his hair, then clawing.

Beast ground out her name in a voice that couldn't pass for human, but it called to her soul. So deep, so perfect, so good. She yelled out his name and arched her back against the mattress as release rippled through her again. Out of her mind with pleasure, she dragged her nails down his back. Beast snarled a sexy, terrifying sound and rammed into her, froze, then shot warmth into her. When he reared back and slammed into her again, there was more warmth. Nothing had ever been like this. No single moment in her life was comparable.

Beast, big, dominant male, wasn't breeding her as he'd no doubt been trained to do.

He was making love to her instead.

Another wave of orgasm blasted through her, and something inside of her ripped apart. A strange noise rattled up her throat, and Beast, with no warning at all, sank his teeth into her shoulder, right over Justin's mark.

It hurt. Oh, it hurt! The shock of it left her breathless, but the pleasure overrode the pain because they were still connected at the hips. Her release still throbbed on with Beast's, creating such an odd, beautiful, all-consuming sensation.

When he let go of her torn skin, a wave of dizziness blasted through Kiera. Her insides were ripping apart, burning, changing, and she closed her eyes against the agony.

This time, she clawed him good because she couldn't help herself, couldn't control her body.

A snarl she didn't recognize ripped through her and then...

Nothing.

With a gasp, Kiera opened her eyes. Beast was up on locked arms, looking down at her with an odd expression, as if he was waiting for something.

"What did you do?" she whispered in horror as warmth streamed from her shoulder.

Beast shook his head, looking utterly confused. "I thought it would work. I could feel her. She was calling me, calling for a bite, begging me to release her." Beast's face went slack when he dragged his golden gaze down her chest to her stomach. His chest heaved and even she, with her duller senses, could feel his panic.

Beast bolted off her and then paced at the foot of the bed, eyes on the swell of her stomach. He ran his hands over and over his short hair. "Kiera?"

She curled up on herself, feeling completely vulnerable under his gaze. "I wanted to tell you."

"No, no, no," he murmured, shaking his head. "How far along?"

"Beast," she whispered, reaching for him.

He jerked backward and slammed his back against the wall. "How far?"

Kiera's throat was tight with emotion as she choked out, "Four months."

Beast gripped the back of his head. His face had turned red in the dim moonlight. He looked gutted. He slammed his head back against the wall. "Human. Kiera tell me it'll be human."

Tears blurred her vision. She didn't understand what was happening, but she understood the bottomless pain in Beast's eyes. "It'll be a lion cub."

"Fffffuck." Beast slid down the wall and squatted on the floor, hands gripping the back of his head. "Who?" When Beast looked up at her, his eyes were rimmed with moisture. "Who fathered it, Kiera."

"Justin Moore of the Tarian Pride."

"Justin Moore," he said in a hollow voice. Fury churned in his eyes.

"You know of him?"

"No, Kiera, I know him. Everything about him. He gave me this." He jammed a finger at his face. "He's the bachelor that got away, and only one because he secured an entire fucking pride under him to protect him from my wrath. I've been waiting for him to fuck up, Kiera. Waiting for him to be outed by another male so I can kill that mother fucker. I can't do it now, or by Lion Law, I would have to take over his pride. He's untouchable, torturing me with every breath he takes. Out of everyone...Justin? He's the father of—he's the—fuck!"

"Oh, my gosh," Kiera whispered.

Beast's fury morphed to panic in an instant. "Kiera, you have to get out!"

"Beast, please. I'm sorry!"

He stood and bolted for the door, but he didn't make it. An enormous lion ripped out of him with such power it blasted her backward on the bed. He rounded on her and charged in the same graceful motion. Beast was shockingly fast. He was a blur, and then he was on her, paws the size of her head on either side of her shoulders, gold eyes locked on her and full of fury. She whimpered and covered her belly protectively, but what could she really do against an animal like this? He was the size of a truck.

"Beast, please. You bit me, remember?" she pleaded in desperation. "Look, I'm still bleeding from your claiming mark. It's me. It's me and you."

He opened his mouth and roared a deafening sound, but she knew he was in there somewhere because he didn't move to hurt her. Terrified, she reached up and ran her palms over his thick, coarse mane. Beast was a beautiful animal. The perfect specimen of dominant alpha lion. Black scars webbed his face, and his ear had a notch taken out of it, but his mane was chestnut-colored and full, his head massive. His teeth were impossibly long and white, his body unimaginably powerful. And his eyes... The anger faded and was replaced by the saddest look she'd ever seen. He looked down at her belly with a slow blink, then slunk off the bed completely. He paced one tight circle, barely able to fit in the small space of the room, then lifted one side of his lip, let off a soft rattling snarl, and walked gracefully from the room.

A howl lifted on the wind, then another, followed by the roar of a grizzly and the scream of a panther.

Holding the sheets around herself, Kiera stood slowly, but hunched when the sound of shattering glass blasted through the trailer. The battle cry of a lion followed within seconds, and Kiera screamed, "Beast, no!" She bolted for the living room, but she could see it from here in the glowing lights of the gazebo.

The D-Team was at war. They were bleeding each other with such frenzied violence Kiera barely felt the shard of glass on the floor that cut her foot as she came to a stop in the middle of the destroyed living room.

The grizzly and Beast's massive lion looked like they were trying to murder each other.

The twin roars of the Blackwing dragons rattled the mountains and shook the floor under her feet.

Kane's Mountains were full of unrest.

And all of this was her fault.

NINE

The roar hadn't been for Kiera. Beast had released the bellow he knew would call the other animals to him. It was a challenge to the D-Team, because right now, he needed to bleed something, and he would kill himself before he drew another drop from Kiera again. The claiming mark had been hard enough.

He needed the wolves, the panther, but most of all, he needed Logan's grizzly. No one had ever been a match like that psychotic ex-mercenary. His animal was an even fight for Beast—broken and empty and only sated by blood.

His world felt like it was collapsing inward as he'd smashed through the front picture window in desperation to engage with the others.

Pregnant. Kiera was his dream girl, perfectly broken into the exact jagged shape that matched his rough edges, and now she was pregnant? God, how badly had he wanted cubs? How desperate had he become to have even one? He'd obsessed over his failures, and here was his match, his mate, his potential *everything*, so unlike any of his pride females. She was enough for him, more than enough, but a cub? Justin had the claim. The Tarian Pride had fucking dibs on that baby, and on Kiera, too.

His claiming mark stood for nothing because that little life in her belly would change into a lion someday.

He'd had hope for a minute! For one blinding moment, he'd convinced himself he could be okay because he wanted to devote his life to making sure Kiera was okay. He wanted to be stronger for her, and it had been so potently life-altering to feel like he had a purpose again.

He'd been a damn caged animal, released into the gorgeous wild, and then shoved into a dark cage and chains again. How could hope hurt this fucking badly?

Make me forget this pain!

Logan was ready for him, his eyes glowing silver as he charged.

A flash of relief washed through him in the instant before he and Logan connected. This was where he belonged—in violence. He could forget everything here. This was his reset. Pain blasted through him as Logan got a claw down his ribs, but Beast was already countering, sinking his teeth into Logan's neck. The roaring and snarling of battle was deafening. No room for inconvenient thoughts of heartbreak here. Just survival.

Dustin was on his back, teeth in his hip, but he wasn't dominant enough to make any real move, so Beast let him chew on him to keep his grip on Logan. Fucking wolf was annoying, though. Winter had both claws in him now, and her teeth pierced his back. Fuck! They were serious tonight.

Beast swung to the side and ducked out of Logan's swatting range. Emma had her teeth sunk into the muscular hump on the brown bear's back, completely locked onto him. The D-Team were trying to split them up and distract them, but it wouldn't work. Not tonight. Logan shook her hard. Beast tried to get back to Logan, but Dustin blocked him, zigzagging back and forth, snarling, snapping his teeth. *Fucking move!*

A dragon roar shook the ground beneath his paws, and another followed immediately. Well, shhhit, he'd only meant to call the D-Team's animals. He had to hurry. Rowan would let them brawl, but Kane would split them up, and Beast wasn't ready to go back to hurting on the inside again yet.

He snarled and rounded on Winter, but he was bigger than her by three times. She backed off quick with a hiss. Smart panther.

Beast charged Logan again after he shook off Emma, and Dustin couldn't stop him this time.

Someone was yelling now. Familiar. Pretty voice. A voice that distracted him and got him a claw to the belly. Logan would gut him if he wasn't careful.

"Beast, stop!"

Fuck Logan, he could feel Beast's claws, feel his teeth, feel his wrath. This was for the fuckers who took everything. Fucking lions. Why was he born to this godforsaken shifter animal? A lineage of killers and barbarians bred generation to generation to annihilate each other, just so they could put their dicks in females.

"Beast!" Beautiful. Beautiful shriek. It was a song he wanted to listen to, and he rounded on her.

She stood there, wrapped in his sheet, skin pale and so perfect, the swell of her little belly pushing against the linens, her hair wild in the wind, tears streaming down her cheeks. Over the scent of blood and anger, he could make out his own smell on her. So thoroughly claimed. But it didn't count.

Now, the pain on his insides matched his outsides as Logan tackled him. Fucking bear stole the beauty from his line of sight. Too heavy. Claws down his back. Fuck you, Logan.

There was fire now. He could smell it, but he didn't give a single shit what the dragons did because Logan had opened himself up, and they would be too late. The grizzly had given him just enough room to twist and reach his soft underbelly.

Now Winter was screaming, too. She'd Changed back too late to change his mind, though. The lion had him. The bloodlust had him.

He sank his teeth into Logan, but didn't get his jaw locked before the massive bear was knocked off of him and into a tree. Furious, Beast righted himself and glared into the green, prehistoric eyes of the demon dragon himself, The Darkness.

Smoke billowed from his nostrils, and his face was so close, Beast could count his teeth behind his snarled, black-scaled lips. His head was the size of Beast's trailer. Anger boiling in his veins, Beast opened his mouth and roared at the monster.

Two clicks of a fire starter sounded, and the scent of fire accelerant filled Beast's senses. Kane reared his long neck back and spewed a line of fire into the air, illuminating the night. Ashes rained down on the trailer park.

Do it! Kill me!

Beast turned and stared at the perfect swell of Kiera's belly. If the baby had been human, he could've had everything.

He'd been so…fucking…close.

Kane might as well light him up and turn him to ashes and dust.

Beast was as good as dead inside anyway.

TEN

Kiera couldn't move. She was trapped in the massive lion's heartbroken gaze. It was clear he wouldn't be able to move past this. He wasn't one of those shifters who could accept another man's child. And it wasn't just another man, either. It was the child of a man who had helped kill his pride and taken everything away from Beast. It was the child of the man who helped to break him.

Her heartbreak was infinite.

Somewhere over the last couple of days, she'd toyed more and more with the idea, pretended perhaps, that she could have everything. That she could keep her baby and be good enough for it. If she had someone like Beast keeping her on the straight and narrow and supporting her, maybe she could be okay at this.

But her first instincts about Beast—and the giant, dominant animal inside of him—were right. He was governed by his animal side. That much was clear by the bloodshed he'd just started. Lions in the wild killed other male's offspring. They couldn't accept cubs with different genetics. And Beast was more animal than man with an acute hatred for Justin.

Everyone was bleeding. The clearing smelled like iron and smoke.

She should be focused on the fire-breathing dark dragon perched above them, but she couldn't take her eyes of Beast. Beautiful, dominant, brawling Beast had just roared a challenge to Kane. A challenge like he'd given the others. She'd watched him spiral. Watched him bleed his crew. Watched him roar for his own death in the face of The End of Days.

He couldn't keep her steady. He couldn't even keep himself steady.

Tears streamed down her cheeks, burning more than they should, as if made of lava. Cradling her belly, she whispered, "Beast, I wanted to tell you, but

I wasn't ready to tell anyone."

Kane backed off, careful not to crush the trailers in the park, stepping gingerly as he snarled a deep rattling sound with every smoky breath. She'd never seen the dragon so in control. The Kane she knew in Apex would've burned Beast to nothing with that challenge.

So, people could change. Just maybe not people like Beast.

Kiera ripped her gaze away from Beast because he was staring at her belly with such fire in his eyes. And yeah, it hurt. It hurt, okay? He looked at her differently. She was a pregnancy now to him, not a person. Not someone beautiful and mysterious and worth getting to know. She'd given away her heart when they were making love and now it felt like he was squeezing it in his hand.

The others were Changing back, so she wiped her eyes. Logan's chest and abs were shredded, and he couldn't stand on his own. Emma and Dustin were trying to get him to his feet, but Winter had other ideas.

Naked, clawed up, and with gold fury in her eyes, Winter ran at Beast. She shoved him so hard she stumbled. "Fuck you, Beast. Fuck you! We were sleeping. We were happy. You ripped our animals out of us, and then you nearly killed him. You nearly killed him, you fucking fuck!" Winter's shoulders shook with her crying, and she shoved him again.

Beast didn't fight it. He let her push him and walked slowly past Kiera toward the woods, each footstep graceful, but heavy as if he shouldered the weight of the world. Perhaps he always had.

Hands touched Kiera's back, and she jumped. It was Rowan looking down at her belly. "You got a baby in you, Kiera?" she asked softly.

Kiera broke down…just…sobbing. It felt so good to have it out there, and so utterly terrible all at once. Rowan hugged her tight, but she could still see him, the shifter she wanted walking away. She watched him until he disappeared into the shadows, and never once did he look back.

A few seconds more, and a long lion bellow sounded, and then another and another. They got shorter and shorter until Beast quit his lament and shrouded the trailer park in silence.

He was just on the edge of the woods, so close…yet completely unreachable.

She was mindless with sadness right now, overwhelmed and overpowered by it. For a moment, she'd felt whole. She'd lost the hollowness. Beast had filled it up, and now she had to go back to being empty again. "I almost had him, Rowan. I almost had everything."

"Shhhh, he just needs some time."

But Rowan didn't understand. Kiera had seen that dead-eyed look in a lion before. She'd seen it on Tammy's face when she told Kiera's social worker she couldn't take her in. It was the look of goodbye.

"Emma, can you get the bleeding stopped?" Rowan asked over Kiera's shoulder.

"I'll do my best," the woman answered. They were trying to get Logan inside the doublewide trailer he shared with his mate, but he was dead weight and not much help. His feet dragged behind them, leaving two lines in the dirt.

Beast had done that. She'd done that.

Kiera was in way over her head here. Too much hung in the balance with these troubled shifters. One argument could spell death for one of them. Or all of them. They'd gone to battle with such single-minded tenacity, it left her shaken.

"Come on," Rowan said, pulling her toward the silver RV. "You're bleeding, too."

Kiera stumbled numbly beside her and stared down at the new claiming mark. What had possessed him to do that? With Justin, she'd begged and begged for the shot to get her animal back like Kane had. He'd been bitten by Rowan, another dragon shifter, and his dragon's return had been immediate.

But with Beast, she hadn't begged. She hadn't pleaded with him to claim her. Hadn't cried to him about the shame she felt when she saw Justin's bite in the mirror every morning. Hadn't asked him to cover it up with one of his own. He'd just done it.

Kiera Pierce—twice claimed, and the keeper of none.

Her face crumpled with her crying as Rowan guided her into the Airstream trailer. The dragon shifter's hands were shaking as she hit the tap water in the tiny kitchen sink. It was brown as it came out and took a few seconds to run clear.

When Rowan pulled a rag from under the sink, her hands were shaking harder, and a soft rumble emanated from her.

Kiera sniffed. "Are you okay?"

The door banked open, startling Kiera, and in walked Kane, clad in jeans and nothing more, looking flushed and still smelling of dragon's fire. His jet black hair hung in front of his face, and when he leaned against the closed door, he looked up and sighed. "Why didn't you tell me you were pregnant, Kiera?"

How did she explain this when she was feeling so vulnerable and raw? She didn't know where to start, so she opened and closed her mouth a couple times in search of the right words.

"I can't have babies," Rowan whispered raggedly. "You probably know this. Kane and I have too much dragon in us, and carrying a pure dragon child would kill me. Do you know this?"

"Yes," Kiera whispered.

"I have expressed interest in a surrogate. Do you also know this?"

"Yes."

Rowan huffed a breath and spun, rested her hands behind her on the edge of the counter. "Why were you stalking us, Kiera? Beast said you were here weeks before you let Kane see you."

"Because I wanted to see if you were the ones. I

don't know if I can do this. I don't know if I can keep the baby and be any good. I was raised by a rogue, and she died early. I couldn't secure a pride, have been stripped of my lioness, and have spiraled my whole life." Kiera wiped her cheeks with the backs of her hands. "I don't want it raised by a pride, and especially not Justin's pride. He's awful, Rowan. No lion other than my mother has ever done anything for me but hurt me." She shrugged and cupped her belly. "Until Beast."

Rowan lifted her chin, and her gold dragon eyes were rimmed with moisture that spilled onto her cheeks. "Winter will be my surrogate. She offered, and the paperwork is done. She's serious about it. If all goes well, she will be having mine and Kane's baby, a dragon at little risk to her, and then she and Logan will be trying for their own cub when she's ready. Kane and I won't be raising your cub, Keira."

A flood of relief washed through her, and Kiera huffed out the breath she'd been holding. The baby fluttered hard in her tummy, and she smiled emotionally down at it. "That's okay," Kiera said, lifting her attention back to Rowan. "I'm happy Winter is going to give you a baby." And she truly was. She'd just grown a huge respect for them, not only for Rowan and Kane, but for Winter and Logan as well.

Rowan's smile was slow and steady, and her nostrils flared, as if scenting the air. "And that reaction right there says you'll do just fine as a mother."

The Second of the Blackwing Crew reached forward and dabbed the washrag onto the bloodied claiming mark. It stung, but not as bad as Kiera had expected. Rowan frowned and eased closer, pressed a bit harder. Her gold eyes twitched to Kiera, then back to the wound, but Kiera understood the bafflement. She wasn't bleeding anymore, and it looked half healed.

"Oh, my God," Rowan said reverently.

"Chills blasted down Kiera's arms. "What's happening?"

Rowan looked over at Kane with eyes as round as moons. And when Kiera followed her gaze, Kane was staring at her claiming mark with the strangest smile on his face.

"You can't Change when you're pregnant, Kiera," he rumbled in a voice that wasn't entirely human yet.

Kiera didn't understand. "I can't Change at all."

Kane's smile widened slightly. "Not yet. You picked wrong with Justin." He nodded his head to the side, toward the woods where Beast had disappeared. "You got it right the second time."

Her shoulders shook when it hit her what he was saying. But oh, she needed to make sure so her hopes didn't get annihilated again. "Just say it," she begged.

Kane stood and limped to her, held her tight, and against her ear, he murmured, "Beast gave you your animal back, Kiera. You smell like a lioness, and you heal like a shifter. Have that baby, and you'll Change again. She's staying quiet so she can protect your cub."

Kiera sagged against him, and a soft wail came from her lips as she cried. And then Rowan was there, hugging her and Kane tight and crying right along with her.

She couldn't believe it. Didn't want to get her hopes up, because what if it wasn't true? But something had clicked into place when Kane had said that. She'd felt her lioness when she and Beast had been together. *Let me show her to you.*

Beast had known exactly what he was doing.

He hadn't just made love to her.

He'd made her whole again.

Kane eased back and released her into Rowan's arms. He pulled a blue folder off the table and returned.

He swallowed hard and dragged his emotional gaze to Kiera's. "I don't know what will happen with Beast. I don't understand the dynamics, and I don't know why he has been putting off pledging to my crew. But whatever happens"—he handed her the folder—"I don't want you to run." The corner of his lip turned up in a sad smile, and then he pulled Rowan's hand, and led his mate out of the trailer.

At the door, Rowan let off this beautiful little sigh and smiled prettily, her eyes so full of emotion. "Kiera, you'll be calling me Roe now. That's what my friends call me. I'm honored you thought of us when you were considering a home for your baby." Her smile dislodged twin tears right before she turned and left the door to swing closed on the RV.

Kiera inhaled deeply as she opened the folder. Inside was the official paperwork for registration to the Blackwing Crew. Stunned, she gently lifted the black bear paw beer bottle opener from the clear sleeve in the center and stared at the Blackwing Crew logo on it.

Beast had made her whole, and the dragons had just offered her a permanent place to grow her roots.

But if she did this—some instinct deep inside of her said it would chase Beast from these mountains. Although that had been the plan to begin with, now, it would rip her heart out to take his home away from him.

She sat heavily on the bed and looked at her name written in purple crayon on the wall.

Perhaps she was meant for a place like this—a home on wheels. Perhaps she was meant to never settle. But Beast, Kane, and this fucked-up crew of monsters made it so tempting to slam on the brakes and stop rolling down the hill of destruction she'd found herself on.

But even if she really, really wanted this, she couldn't push out Beast. He'd been through hell, and he'd chosen this place for sanctuary. She couldn't take that away from him.

Kiera gripped the bottle opener hard in one hand and with the other, she traced her name that Dustin had written on the wall with her fingertip.

It was time to own every bad thing that had happened and start looking toward a better future for this child, for her, and for Beast, because she couldn't give up on him. Not after what he'd been through, and what he'd given her. Not after she'd seen the good parts of him he'd only shared with her.

Kiera sighed and glared at her name on the wall with newfound determination.

It was time to step up and see a wily werewolf about a plan.

ELEVEN

Beast maneuvered the arm of the excavator and dumped another load of mine dirt into the back of the dump truck.

"Are you just going to ignore me all day?" Kane asked testily from where he stood beside the machine.

"Well, that's the beauty of not being officially registered to the crew yet. I don't have to answer your questions."

"I can order you to."

Fucking dragon had a point. Beast snarled his lip at him, blasted the claws of the bucket back into the black earth, and scooped another load into the back of the truck.

"So she's pregnant," Kane said from below. "It's not the end of the world. It could be a good thing."

Beast swung the giant metal arm away from the truck and cut the engine. Pissed beyond belief, Beast jumped out of the machine and scaled the side of the dump truck to pull the tarp over the back. "It'll be a lion cub."

"And you're a lion. I can't think of a better man to show him or her how to navigate this life, Beast."

"It's not mine, Kane! It belongs to one of the fucking *murderers* of my pride!"

Kane readjusted his white hard hat and spat in the dirt. "Maybe if you give it some time, that won't matter so much."

Beast snarled when he passed Kane. Asshole had just come out to the mine site to piss him off and make assumptions about shit he didn't know anything about. The dragon pulled himself up into the passenger's seat too fast for Beast to leave his ass on the mountain. Beast shifted to first and eased the truck onto the steep mountain road that would lead down to the gem mine, newly named The Dragon's Treasure. Clever. Kane had bought the place from the last owner and now was advertising the black dragon inside of him. Smart marketing, actually. Tourists came from all over, not only to mine the beryl, corundum, and sometimes even rubies from the mine dirt, but also to meet Dark Kane, the last Blackwing Dragon on earth. They got to shake the hand of the Apocalypse. Business had been booming.

"That baby won't belong to a crew, Kane. He's property of the pride he was conceived in."

"Property," Kane repeated softly.

"Yep, Lion Law. We have an entire council devoted to making sure everyone follows the rules."

"Kiera doesn't want the baby raised in that pride."

"Great. I wish her wants mattered to the council, but they don't. She's a lioness."

"Jesus."

"You think I don't know how fucked up that is, Kane? Huh? I do! I treated my females like queens, but not every pride is like that. Very few are, actually, and the Tarian Pride? Biggest pride since mine, and all run by a monster, Kane. She picked a monster!"

"Your monster could match him."

"Don't fuckin' tempt me, Dragon. Challenging Justin means I die or I take over his pride. The timing's off. You know my story. Surely you can understand why I want nothing to do with running a pride again."

"You should talk to Kiera, Beast."

"I'm not exactly in the right state of mind to have an intelligent conversation about this. All I can think of—the only thing—is hunting Justin. And for what? So I can keep his claim? So I can keep his kid? I'm supposed to wait, Kane! I'm supposed to hunt him when he isn't an alpha anymore. Going to war with him means going to war with his females, and I'm not doing the same shit he did to me and my pride. I'm not doing it! And now Kiera—*my mate*—is carrying his baby. Fuck," he uttered as he felt socked in the gut. "I won't have anything good to say to her right now. I just need a minute to wrap my head around everything that's happened."

"This isn't a pride, Beast."

"No shit."

"No…I mean…if Kiera doesn't want to raise her baby in a pride, I don't care about Lion Law. She was like a little sister to me once, Beast. I watched her break." His voice cracked on the last word, and the dark-headed alpha slammed his head back on the seat. Softly, he repeated, "I watched her break. Watched them all break in that goddamned facility, but Kiera was different. She'd just lost her mom, just been rejected by the pride who could've saved her lion, and she wasn't fighting the process. She went into the testing rooms hollow looking, like she was already walking through life as a ghost, and she was fifteen years old. There were two extremes in Apex. Kids who gave up too quick—they died. Kids who fought too hard to keep their animal—they died, too. Kiera came in dead-eyed. Do you understand what I'm telling you? The lions didn't do shit for her, so if she doesn't want to raise that little cub in a pride, I give zero fucks."

"What are you saying?"

Kane rolled his head toward Beast. "Screw pride rules, Beast. You aren't in a pride anymore, and Kiera never belonged to one. If she wants in the Blackwings, she'll have my blessing, and she'll have my fire, too, but I know her. You're the obstacle now."

Beast frowned. He didn't understand what that meant. He wasn't anyone's obstacle to anything. He wasn't chasing her out. He just couldn't be around her right now without hurting her feelings. He'd done this shit before. Females were sensitive. Anytime his pride had gone at each other's throats, he'd had to tiptoe around like he was in a fucking minefield.

He didn't know what to say to Kiera. She had a claiming mark from Justin, was carrying his child. She didn't belong to Beast, and what could he really do if the pride came for her? Nothing. And if he tried, they could kill her, and the council would look the other way. For abandoning Justin, the council would consider the punishment justified. Cubs were everything to lions. She had a brick of gold in her belly, and she'd picked one psychotic pride to conceive in. The second Justin found out she was carrying his cub, he would have her, or no one would.

Beast was a broken rogue responsible for the deaths of his entire pride. He wouldn't be responsible for Kiera's death, too.

Kane preached about his fire belonging to Kiera if she needed it, but the dragon didn't understand. He hadn't been raised around the different shifter cultures. He'd grown up alone. Lions weren't like the other shifters. They had their own set of rules and policed themselves, and as much as Kiera wanted to stay rogue, the tiny life inside of her made her a

Tarian by technicality.

Beast had bonded to her, but he'd never really had a shot at making her his.

He gritted his teeth against the pain that unfurled in his middle. The urge to Change was so strong he shook his head hard to rattle the lion off his mission. And as he rounded the last turn in the dirt road, salvation came in the strangest form.

Dustin stood leaned against his black sports car, face in a serious frown for once. Emma stood on the other side, her chin resting on her arms on the roof of the car. Her face was unreadable.

Beast pulled to a stop and rolled down the window. "What?"

"Emma has an appointment with the ear doc up in Asheville. She needs new hearing aids. The others don't work for her very well after she went wolf." Dustin shrugged and stared at the new sign on the main building of Kane's gem mine. "I figured maybe you would want to come to Asheville with us. Stay in a hotel a couple nights, get away, get your head on straight."

Beast huffed a soft, single laugh at the joke, but Dustin wasn't smiling. "Are you serious?"

Dustin scratched the sandy blond scruff on his jaw and gave him his lightened blue and green eyes. "Last night was bad, Beast. You almost killed Logan, and I saw your face when you challenged Kane. You were off the rails." Dustin nodded his chin to his car. "Get in."

In general, Beast didn't like to be told what to do, and especially not by some smartass submissive werewolf, but Dustin was offering him something he couldn't turn down. He was offering him an out. A distraction. An escape from the body-wracking pain that washed over him every time he thought about going back to the trailer park and having *the talk* with Kiera. He wasn't ready to let her go, so okay.

Beast threw the truck into park and climbed out.

"Are you serious?" Kane asked.

"I need a couple days off work."

"Beast—"

"It's this, or I break now," Beast said from where he stood on the ground below. "I want to keep her, Kane. I want to keep Kiera for a couple more days, even if it's just in my head."

"Don't worry, Alpha. I'll keep our resident psychopath from hunting Daddy Lion," Dustin promised Kane. Like he knew everything. Little pissant was annoying for thinking he knew Beast's mind. He did, but still. It was obnoxious that he couldn't just keep it to himself.

Beast snapped his teeth at Dustin as he approached the car. *Move*. But when the wolf didn't jump back or get out of the way for Beast to climb in the back, Beast knew something was up. Dustin smelled off. Nervous. What the fuck was going on?

Beast strode around the front of the car, his suspicious glare on the back of Dustin's head. Emma let him in just fine, and as he began to maneuver his giant frame into the back seat, the roar of the dump truck accelerating drowned out everything. He got about halfway in before her scent hit him like a ton of bricks. Kiera.

Beast paused, halfway in, halfway out of the car.

"Get in quick before Kane sees me," she murmured. Her voice was hollow, dead-sounding, and she looked like she'd been crying. Shhhit.

Beast rattled off a growl and sank into the seat beside her. His shoulders took up two thirds of the back, but she was much smaller than him, so he wasn't squishing her. Yet. Dustin would probably drive like a bat out of hell and have Beast scrabbling for purchase so he wouldn't hurt Kiera and the…the…baby.

Kane had pulled the truck up to the building, so Dustin and Emma got in and shut their doors in a rush.

"What's going on?" Beast ground out, looking at the back of the seat, out the window, at his clenched hands in his lap—anywhere but at Kiera. She smelled so sad.

Fix her.

Beast shook his head as a wave of dizziness blasted through his skull that was followed with a piercing pain behind his eyes. Stupid lion was scratching at his skin, threatening to rip out of him again. Today had been a pill.

"We're going to Asheville," Dustin explained innocently. "You have a two o'clock meeting tomorrow with one mega-chode lion shifter named Justin, which by the way, I hate that his name rhymes with my name because he really is the world's biggest shit-flake."

Beast canted his head at the stupid death-wish-having werewolf. "You put together a meeting with

Justin." It wasn't a question. He had no doubt Dustin somehow thought this was a good idea. "And you just lied to Kane about what we're doing."

"Nope!" Dustin clipped out as he pulled onto the main road. "My moral compass is still broken and pointed due-south, but I haven't quite honed my lying skills when it comes to the dragon. We did make an appointment at the ear doc so I wouldn't have to lie. I just omitted some of the truths."

Beast huffed a breath and shook his head, rested his elbow on the window and bit his thumbnail. "Does Justin know about the cub?" he asked Kiera. Because if he did, Kiera was already chained to the damn Tarian Pride.

"Yes. He could tell before I even knew." She sounded terrified, as she should be. "He doesn't know where I am, but I know he's looking. I've been on the move to stay ahead of him."

Fuck, fuck, fuckety, fuck. "There will be no good outcome to doing this. He'll take you away."

Something slapped against his leg. It was a blue folder Kiera had tossed onto his lap. When he looked up at her, Kiera's eyes were rimmed with tears.

She inhaled a trembling breath and jammed her

finger at it. "Everything I didn't even have the imagination to dream of is in that folder, Beast. I came here to see if I could give my baby away to the dragons, so it wouldn't be raised in that awful pride. I talked to Kane and Rowan about it last night, and they gave me an option that's so much more than I deserve, but that I want really, really badly. I want to be a Blackwing, but even more than that, I want you to stay and try for the same because you deserve this, too. But I know we can't move past this until it's all in the open. I don't want us living our whole lives wondering what if. I don't know your heart, Beast. I only know mine, and I would wonder for always what we could've been, because I truly, deeply care for you. So much it scares me. If you can't accept this child, tell me now, and we'll go back to the trailer park, and I'll pack my shit and leave. If your animal can't get past it, lay it out there right now so I can try to move on. But if there is a way that you could still care for me despite what I used to think was a mistake but is now something I truly love..." Kiera wrapped her arms around her little stomach and looked so beautiful. Like a goddess. Like everything he wanted. "Then we'll go, and I'll beg Justin to let me live my life the way I want to, with you. With the Blackwings. I'll plead on my knees if I have to."

Beast snarled at the thought of his queen on her knees. He would bleed the entire fucking pride before he saw her bow to them.

She didn't know what she was really asking. It wouldn't be a clean break. Justin wouldn't let her go, no matter how much anyone groveled. Beast knew what it took to run a pride that size. It took lethal decision-making skills and a darkness of the heart. And he'd seen the emptiness in Justin's eyes the night he went to war with his pride. He killed females like they were nothing. Kiera had given him simple choices—tell her he couldn't get past the baby's parentage and move on, or fix this for her. She had it wrong, though. She wouldn't be begging her freedom. Instead, she would be the single bullet in the chamber that would incite war between Kane's Mountains and the lions.

Kiera looked gorgeous, staring at him with open, vulnerable blue eyes—blue now because her lioness wasn't some dead thing inside of her anymore. Beast had released her, just like she deserved, which wouldn't have worked if Kiera didn't love him. It wouldn't have worked if she didn't see him as her mate.

Fuck, she was his *mate*. A single mate. Lions weren't supposed to do that—choose one. But silverbacks weren't either, and Callum had picked one mate, even though he was supposed to be in charge of a family group. Was it that unbelievable that Beast had bonded to Kiera after watching Callum devote himself entirely to one woman? Hell no. Beast was following a similar path in his search for happiness, and maybe two years ago, when he was king of his territory and had the world at his feet, that would've bothered him. But now, he had nothing but the Blackwings and Kiera…and that tiny bump pushing against her fitted sweater dress.

Dustin pulled to a stop at a T in the road. One way led back to Kane's Mountains, one to the highway. "What'll it be, Beast-Man?" Dustin asked softly. "Ashville or the trailer park to say goodbye."

Beast watched Kiera's face as he answered, "The trailer park." Heartbreak slashed through her eyes for a moment before he continued. "I'll be driving us to Ashville, just Kiera and me. This is lion business—"

"No, this is crew business," Dustin argued. He

smelled pissed. "I set up this meeting. I'm going as your backup."

"You'll stay here with your mate and wait for us to come back, and you won't utter a word of this to the D-Team because I can't join the crew until I fix this."

Dustin shook his head and twisted in his seat, "But Beast—"

"Dustin, I'm saving your life because you're my friend."

Dustin froze, and then his mouth flopped open.

"I'll bring her back," Beast promised. God, he hoped he could follow through. "But Justin won't come alone, and you'll be used as leverage. You're a submissive werewolf. You'll be a target, and I can't keep my head where it needs to be if I'm pulled in different directions. Do you understand?"

Dustin nodded once, gripped the steering wheel with one hand, and took a right toward Kane's Mountains.

Kiera's hand slid over Beast's tense thigh, and he rolled his eyes closed at how good it felt to have her touch him again. He sighed and lifted his arm over her, pulled her in close against his ribs, and kissed the top of her head as he watched the Smoky Mountains blur by the window. Or at least he tried. Beast couldn't help that his attention dipped time and time again to her stomach. She wasn't wearing the baggy sweaters anymore to conceal her pregnancy, but something form-fitting instead. He wanted to touch her but was hesitant. Kiera seemed to know just what he needed and pulled his hand slowly over the curve of her tummy and pressed his palm there with hers, just held him as she looked up into his eyes. In this moment—the one where he touched not only his mate but the life she carried too—everything changed.

He'd never wanted anything more than what he had right here.

Silently, Beast swore an oath to himself that he would make her life safe again, no matter the cost to him.

He'd lost everything once, and he couldn't do that again. He wouldn't survive it.

His real options were to walk away from the woman he loved and leave her unprotected, or go to war with her pride for her freedom.

War it was.

TWELVE

Kiera watched the night woods blur by the highway. It had taken a while to pack and load up Beast's truck, and they'd stopped to eat dinner, so now it was late to be driving to Asheville. She liked the slower pace, though, because it meant she got more quality time with Beast.

"I've done this before," Beast murmured over the soft hum of rock music that drifted through the stereo speakers.

Kiera reached forward and turned down the music. He hadn't spoken for a while and had seemed lost in thought, so she didn't want to miss any of this conversation. "You've done what before?" Kiera asked, holding tighter to his hand. She'd been clingy because she was scared, but he wasn't balking against her touch anymore.

"One of my pride females got pregnant."

"What?" she asked, shocked.

"I was five years into my rein, and she was a little thing. Petite for a lioness. Fine-boned, submissive. She told me the second she suspected it, and I was so scared to hope that we kept it to ourselves. We didn't want to get the other female's hopes up that maybe I wasn't...you know." *Sterile.*

Kiera lifted his hand to her cheek and let it rest there. "What happened?"

"Alisha went to the doctor. The pregnancy was confirmed, and I was just..." Beast shook his head and had this faraway smile as he blew down Interstate 74. "I was so fuckin' happy. And it wasn't about not being a failure anymore. I was just so happy I was gonna be a dad. I had all these imaginings of little league baseball games, birthday parties, and first day of school pictures. I had it in my head it was a boy. I was gonna raise him to be a good lion, like Callum had raised me. I was gonna teach him how to survive this life. I was gonna take care of him. I bought this little outfit. *Daddy's little manimal* was written across the front. And it had a picture of this cartoon lion on the butt. Cutest fuckin' thing you've ever seen. Tiny. I would pull it out and just sit on the bed and hold that little outfit in my hands and imagine what it would be like holding my son. I thought about naming him after the man who stepped in and raised me." Beast inhaled deeply and expelled the breath. "We planned a party to tell the rest of the pride, but two days before, Alisha started bleeding." Beast opened his mouth, but nothing came out. He swallowed hard and shook his head.

Kiera laid tiny kisses on his knuckles as her heart broke for him.

"The way I reacted when I found out you were pregnant..." He gave her a raw look that pleaded understanding. "It wasn't that I was angry that it was another man's baby, Kiera. I mean, I would've loved that for us. I would've loved for you to carry my child someday. The anger wasn't about that though. It was that I could see I was going to go through the same thing again. I was going to get my hopes up, and the baby would be taken away. And you..." Beast swallowed hard before he continued. "You were going to be taken away because of the baby."

"I didn't think I wanted to be a mother," she admitted in a whisper.

Beast tossed her a frown, but she couldn't hold his gaze so she gave her attention to tracing figure 8s around his knuckles. "Apex did something awful to my insides, Beast. I have no gauge for normal. They messed with my brain." She gestured to the side of her head with the scars that were hidden by her hair. "My memories of my life before are blurry now. I forgot a lot about my mom. Memories I wanted to keep forever got jumbled the more experiments they did. I would stay awake at nights and repeat memories over and over so I could try to keep them. I would think of my mom's smile a hundred times before I went to sleep. That was the ritual, so I could keep her, because I could feel my lioness fading every day. They said I was the fastest cleanse they'd ever done, like it was some good thing. Something to brag about. Something that deserved a pat on the back. My lioness gave up the fastest. I gave up the fastest. I thought if I didn't fight, I would get to keep more of my mom." She pressed her lips against the back of his strong hand.

"Did you?"

She shook her head. "I didn't want to be a mom because I couldn't remember all the good stuff my mom did for me, and I was convinced that I wouldn't have the right instincts to be a good one. Not after Apex. But then I got pregnant. I saw that test, and it was positive. I waited for the freak-out. I waited for that gut-wrenching *I've made a mistake* feeling, but it never came. I was overcome with this protectiveness instead. I wanted the baby to have the best life, even if that didn't include me. What could I do against Justin and an entire pride? I can't even Change to protect my child. I felt like I couldn't do this on my own. I wasn't enough on my own to protect the baby from the Tarian Pride. I ran from Chicago, away from Justin's reach within three days of that first test, and I've been at war with myself ever since."

"About whether to keep it?"

"Yeah. It tortured me—the back and forth. But then I met you, and everything happened so fast."

"What do you mean?"

"I mean the feelings. I thought it was hormones at first, but there was something about you from the first second I saw you that terrified me and made you so unavoidable all at once. I couldn't stop thinking about you. You were so, sooo different from what I'd heard about. You're good, Beast."

"I'm not."

"You are. And you're good for me. I made my decision." She pulled his hand over her belly again. He couldn't seem to stop touching it anyway. "I want to keep it. I want to raise it. And I want you to be there. You feel important to me. You make me feel safe, and for me, that's a really big deal, Beast."

"You are safe, Kiera. You both are." His voice rang with such honesty, she smiled. Plus, she didn't know if he realized it, but he was gently rubbing her belly, back and forth, back and forth. The baby was going crazy. It felt like a swarm of bats in her stomach right now, and it tickled.

She giggled, and a big kick bumped right where Beast's hand was. Kiera gasped. "Please tell me you felt that."

Beast had frozen right where it had hit, and he looked at her with such a shocked face, she couldn't help her breathless laugh.

"Was that a kick?" he asked.

"It was! I haven't felt any on the outside yet, but that was a big one. You felt it?"

"I definitely felt something. It was like…" He grinned so big. "It was like feeling a single little heartbeat against my hand.

The bats were fluttering again. "It's still kicking!"

Beast took an exit off the highway and maneuvered the truck onto an old one-lane road, his palm firm against her belly as he drove his Raptor with one hand. "Hang on, hang on, hang on," he murmured distractedly, pulling over to the side of the dark road. "Come here," he said, shoving his seat back as far as it went.

With a squeak, Kiera let him guide her over the console and onto his lap. She was wearing a sweater dress, so she pulled it up above the curve of her stomach and placed his hands on either side of her belly, just under her ribs. Beast was staring at her stomach as though mesmerized, stroking his thumbs softly against her taut skin. "I got to feel the first outside kick?" he asked.

Kiera nodded. Her face hurt from smiling so big. She'd never in a million years thought she was going to share a moment like this with someone, and now she was here with Beast.

The fluttering intensified, and then there was

another big bump. Beast missed it, but she pulled his hand over fast, right near her belly button, and there was another hard kick.

Beast went rigid, spine straight like he'd been electrocuted. His gaze collided with hers. "I felt it," he whispered in awe. "That's a baby."

Excitedly, Kiera bounced up and down on his lap and grabbed his shoulders, shook him gently. "I've been waiting so long for outside kicks!"

"Here," he murmured, pulling her hand over the spot he'd felt the last one. He pressed her fingertips there and studied her face as they both waited. The baby kicked on the other side, just out of her range. With a gasp, she chased it, and he followed, palm firm on top of hers.

The baby kicked again, and this time she felt it. This was everything. Sitting here in the truck, straddling the man she loved, chasing baby kicks with soft rock playing in the background and that stunning smile on Beast's face.

"Maybe the baby was waiting for me to make my decision before it kicked like this," she whispered.

"Or maybe you just needed to drink those four large glasses of orange juice at dinner," Beast teased.

She nudged him in the arm and tried to look severe. "It was fresh-squeezed, and I was thirsty."

"Mmm, and now I'm thirsty," he murmured, leaned forward into her. He sucked gently on her neck.

Kiera's body turned to water. It was waves, and Beast was the moon, controlling her movement. Chasing his warmth, her skin stayed on his as he eased back. With a happy sigh, she slid her arms over his shoulders, arched her back, and pressed against him. She'd almost lost this connection. She'd come so close to having to compare any man who followed to Beast. He trailed his fingertips down her throat, to her collar bone, to her breast. His lips were so soft against her neck—hard suck, soft kiss, hard suck. He wasn't rushing them, no. He was making sure she knew he adored her—by touch.

The road was dark and some distance off the interstate. It was surrounded by shadowed woods, but still, Kiera didn't want to be caught in a compromising position. Visions of police officers with flashlights knocking on the steamed-up window flashed through her mind as she glanced up the road to make sure they were safe.

"Eyes on me," Beast murmured against her neck. How had he known? Perhaps he could now sense her focus. Was that what bonds did? She could definitely feel something coming from him. Happiness? Did a broken man like Beast know that emotion? God, she hoped so, and she hoped she was the one who helped him keep it.

Beast trailed his sucking kisses to the other side of her throat. He would make bruises if she were still human, but already, Kiera could feel the hickey's cooling as though she'd put ice on them. Another wave of relief washed over her, and with the emotion came a soft sound from deep down inside of her.

It was a rattling sound that pulsed in waves, louder then softer. She was purring for the first time since her animal had been taken from her. Wild lions couldn't make this sound, but shifters could. *She* could.

Beast stilled against her, and his lips curved into a smile against her neck. "There you are," he murmured.

Her sweater dress had a deep V at the neck, and Beast curled his fingers into the opening and yanked it to the side. When he cupped her breast, she arched against him again. He wasn't even touching skin since the lace of her bra separated them, but she was so sensitive. The shoulder of her dress was dragged down her arm, exposing her skin to the air. Where Beast trailed fire with his fingertips, his lips followed, kissing her gently down her neck to the tip of her collarbone. Kiera was panting already. The man still had on all his clothes, but he'd seduced her entirely, body and soul. Desperation clawed at her heart to be closer to him, but it warred with letting him take control. She'd always been on her own, unsafe, uncared for, and here was this giant of a man, more animal than anything else, who was making sex easy. *So* easy. So enjoyable. No thinking required on her part, he was leading. All she had to do was follow.

Beast eased back and teased her with an almost kiss that had her chasing his lips. He was smiling such a wicked expression she couldn't look away from him now if she tried. *Eyes on me.*

He began to pull the other side of her dress down her shoulder and dragged his gaze away from hers, eyes following his own fingertips as he slid it from her skin. "So soft," he whispered. His touch left her skin, but not for long. Beast traced her new claiming mark scar. "Soft but not fragile."

He cupped the back of her neck and dragged her forward until his lips were right over his bite mark. His hands went to her hips, and now he was smiling against her skin again. Maybe because she sighed out a helpless sound when his hands touched the sensitive skin over her ribs.

A soft snarl rattled in his throat. Sexy, and probably as close to a purr as a feral man like Beast would ever get. Kiera wanted to feel it. With trembling fingers, she lifted the hem of his black sweater. His abs flinched at her touch, and the snarl in his throat kicked up a notch, but the devilish glint in his gold eyes said it wasn't a bad thing. Maybe he would always be surprised by touch. Kiera returned his naughty smile and dragged her nails up his torso slowly as she lifted his shirt. He kissed her, hands sliding up her back to her bra. The sharp *snick* of her bra being released was an extra note in the soft song that played. His lips moved against hers so smoothly, as if he already knew what she liked. God, she loved how confident he was. Only when he'd pushed his tongue past her lips and brushed it against hers enough times to get her heart pounding did he ease back and allow her to pull his sweater over his head the rest of the way. He slid his hand into her loose bra, and cupped her breast as his lips collided with hers again, more urgent, more demanding. The snarl in his throat was louder now, as was the purr in hers. Hard and soft. Beast was harsh and rough around the edges. He was a stony wall of muscle, where she was curves. He was a wild animal, and she was steady. He was the storm, and she was the quiet.

Overcome with emotion, she whispered between kisses, "I love you."

He didn't respond with words, and she hadn't expected him to. Instead, he eased back and searched her eyes, and then slowly, he dragged her palm right over his pounding heartbeat. It was racing so fast as his chest heaved with his quickened breath. The snarl softened under her touch.

Kiera smiled because she understood.

"Want to feel you," he rumbled, hooking his fingers into the front of her panties. "You wet for me yet, Kiera?"

"Always."

He let off a groan as he slid his fingers down her wet folds. "Fffuck."

Riip. Riip.

Kiera stared in shock as her favorite pair of panties hit the passenger's seat in a tiny pile of shredded material. "Monster," she accused him.

"Mmm hmm," he agreed, hooking his hands behind her knees and jerking her forward, closer to his hips.

His lips were everything. All-consuming, sucking, biting her bottom lip, tongue stroking into her mouth. How had she lived up until this point without these feelings? Happy, safe, taken care of...whole. She'd been half a person, and Beast had just come into her life and shoved himself into the spaces left vacant by the grit of her life. He'd stopped the hemorrhaging, stopped the hurt, just by being his complicated, sexy, dominant, sweet-on-the-inside self.

His chest was so firm under her hands. Beast huffed a breath as she reached his abs and punched out a sharp breath when she hooked her fingers into his jeans. How was he so warm? His skin was on fire, but the weather outside chilled her body. He was summer and she was winter, and she was desperate to end the chill. She rolled her hips and brushed her chest against his. His kisses were hard now, desperate. Her lips were throbbing under his demanding affection. He was burning her up, igniting her, setting her insides on fire to match his. Fingers fumbling, she ripped at the button of his jeans and pulled the zipper down, but she clearly wasn't moving fast enough since Beast lifted his hips off the seat and shoved his own pants down his thighs.

There was a moment of hesitation where she sat frozen, staring at his thick erection. Was it even bigger than last time? There was no way the physics were going to work with her on top. But when Beast took himself in hand and pulled a seductive stroke, a challenge in his gleaming eyes, Kiera gave an internal nod. Okay then, this was happening. *Relax.*

She lifted up on her knees and slid shallowly over him. Beast gripped her hips and rested his head back against the seat. His fingers dug into her hips as she pulled off him and then eased down farther. Beast's face was a mixture of pleasure and pain, as if her slow pace was torture. She smiled. Her turn.

Kiera slid her arms around his neck and lifted herself eyelevel with him, then slid onto him again as she kissed him, bit him, licked him. The snarl in his throat jacked up, but so what? She liked him wild. She liked him desperate because it made her feel the same way. She was tight. He liked it, she could tell, because every time she lowered onto him, he tensed up and made a helpless sound deep in his throat. It would've been inaudible to her human self, but she could hear better now that he'd given her animal back. He smelled like rutting male lion, but wasn't turning her over and biting the back of her neck as he unloaded into her. He was here, with her, staying in the moment, letting her lead. Beast had been king of the lions, and he was letting her—a medium dominance female—set the pace.

He may as well have said he loved her too with this move. Kiera took all of him on the next stroke and sped up. She was already so close. This position meant he was hitting her clit every thrust, and now he was meeting her hips, crashing against her, hands strong on her. Desperation looked good on Beast.

"Shit, Kiera, tell me you're close. I can't stop," Beast snarled, hands on her hips as he yanked her onto him harder, faster.

The gravel in his voice did her in. The first pulse of release was so explosive she screamed out his name. On the second, she set her teeth to him, daring herself. Beast was slamming into her now. He grabbed the back of her neck. "Do it quick, I'm coming." Beast rammed into her again and groaned, and this was it. Before she could stop her animal, she sank her teeth into his shoulder. It happened fast, a bite down and release, but it was enough. She'd been thorough. Her lion hadn't been playing around, and the air smelled like pennies. Beast hadn't even flinched, but she didn't want to look at what she'd done because she never wanted to hurt him, so Kiera buried her face against the uninjured side of his neck and gave herself to the orgasm that was blasting through her, spurred on by his deep, graceful strokes inside her.

He drew out every single aftershock from her as he emptied himself completely, filling her with warmth until it spilled from her body. So much. They'd finished so hard. She relaxed against him until her release was completely through.

Emotional beyond words at what she'd just done, she hugged him tightly. "I'm sorry," she murmured.

"Don't, Kiera. Don't take that away from me with an apology." There was a smile in his voice. A smile?

She eased back and frowned at him. His hair was mussed, his face flushed, chest heaving, his shoulder streaming red, and what was he doing? Sitting there with the cockiest grin she'd ever seen on a man.

Unable to help herself, she giggled.

Beast's gold gaze dipped to her lips, and he ran his thumb against her mouth. He drew it back and showed her the smear of red. "Who's the monster now?"

"Me," she squeaked.

Beast licked the blood off his thumb and then kissed her until the taste of it went away. Easing back, he murmured, "Now we match."

But for the life of her, she couldn't figure out if he meant their claiming marks matched or their inner monsters did. Either way drew another smile from her lips.

"Can I tell you something?" he murmured, sweeping her hair back from her face. He looked so damn perfect in the glow of the radio, his eyes muddy bluish gold, teeth sharper than they should've been, face feral, blond hair in that just-woke-up look, muscles rippling, tattoos, scars... perfection.

"You can tell me anything," she said honestly.

"Last night, when we were together for the first time..."

"Yeah?"

"I never claimed anyone but you, Kiera. And I never had sex with a woman like that."

"You mean like you weren't fucking her?"

"Yeah."

"You mean like we just did?"

Beast nodded his chin. "Yesterday when I...you know...knelt at your altar."

Kiera burst out into a giggle. "You can call it eating me out."

Was Beast blushing? "Well, I hadn't done that before either."

"Bull. Shit," she challenged him. "I mean, I can hear you telling the truth, but it has to be a trick or something. Beast, you were so..." *Amazing, confident, mind-blowing.* Kiera cleared her throat delicately. "Skilled."

Beast chuckled and stroked his thumbs over her belly. "Well, you're good at telling me when you like something. You're noisy."

"We're good at this together!" she crowed happily. "Go team!" She raised her hand for a high five, but Beast pulled her wrist to his lips and bit gently. "I'm not giving you a high five for what we just did like we're college roommates, Kitty. High fives are for quickie fucks. We do it better."

"Kitty," she repeated the nickname through a grin. She *was* a kitty because she had her lioness back! She wanted to dance. Dance! She wanted to have a dance party right here on his dick, but put in a real effort not to wiggle around and hurt him. She squealed happily instead and buried her face against his chest.

Beast chuckled a deep rich sound that she adored. That sound sang to her heart. Beast wasn't a laugher, but with her, he was different. He loosened up and smiled more, and now he was giving her chuckles? He'd told her a dozen times tonight that he loved her, too, without words, and this was another one. Every time he laughed like this—so easily—he was admitting his feelings for her, and she knew down to her marrow they were every bit as deep as hers.

She was purring again, loud, soft, loud, soft. "I missed this sound so bad," she whispered.

"Listen closer," Beast said in that velvet-meets-gravel voice of his.

She opened her senses and listened as hard as she could. And just there above the sound of her own purring, another content sound vibrated the air. Kiera frowned. Was that...

She lurched back and studied Beast. His eyes were a piercing blue now, and his smile slight, but relaxed. He lifted her palm to his chest again. There was his pounding heartbeat, but this time there was something more.

He wasn't snarling.

He was purring, too.

His smile widened, and he looked so breathtakingly perfect, scars and all. "Our animals are talking."

Oh, how he ripped her heart open with those four words. They *were* talking. Beast was right. Her animal could've been angry. She had every right to be. She could've burst out of her the second Beast had given her the claiming mark. Her lioness could've shredded her body, hurt the pregnancy, and not given Kiera back her human skin for days. Weeks even. But she hadn't. Beast had brought her back gently, bonded them, and her inner animal was drawn up, eyes on him, steady, protecting the baby, protecting Kiera, protecting Beast. Loving the beast.

"You know you gave me everything, right?" she said thickly. She was determined not to cry again because Beast deserved a strong mate.

His eyes softened, and he pulled her against him, ran his cheek along her face, his whiskers feeling so good against the scars under her hair. He was giving her the affection that lions did when they were happy.

Dominant, brawling man didn't care that she was all jagged edges and missing pieces. *We match.*

Kiera hugged him hard, so tight, and she never wanted to let go of this moment.

Beast sighed and rested his lips right next to her ear. "Tomorrow, when we meet Justin, everything will be okay. I know you're scared. I can feel it." He shook his head. "You don't need to be, Kiera. No matter what, I'll make sure you're safe."

She hadn't missed it, though. He hadn't promised his own safety. Only hers.

"We can run away," she whispered. "We don't have to do this. I can change my mind."

Beast's hand was gentle as he cupped her cheek

and wrapped his other arm tightly around her. How could they be talking about Justin, yet Beast still made her feel safe and warm?

"No more running, Kiera." He kissed her temple and let his lips linger there for a few moments before he whispered, "Not for either of us."

THIRTEEN

Beast eased his Raptor into the parking lot of a hotel. He'd called earlier and booked a nice one. Kiera deserved nice things. He pulled into the circle drive and considered using the valet services immediately, but decided against it. The reason? Kiera was curled up in a little ball, hugging his arm, and sleeping so peacefully. She'd been like this for the last hour.

She'd told him once that she had trouble sleeping because she didn't feel safe. But here she was, sleeping so soundly she didn't even stir when he cut the engine. Beast shook his head at the valet who was giving him a questioning look from his stand. He didn't want to do anything but sit here for a minute and watch her.

He'd spent so much time making sure his pride felt safe under him. Countless brawls and challenges had happened over the ten years he reigned, and he'd always prided himself that his females were safe. That they lived without fear. And then the bachelors had killed everyone. They'd even killed him on the inside. Not a single piece of him ever thought he had a shot at finding what Kiera was offering him. Companionship, love, someone to walk this crazy life with, to grow old with, and on top of it all, along with her own heart, she was offering this tiny miracle that moved in her belly.

Unable to help himself, Beast inhaled deeply and palmed her belly. There was a tiny heartbeat in there. A tiny person. A tiny baby, growing by the day. Kiera was going to be really good at this. He could tell because she was patient, accepting, and kind in ways he'd never seen in other lionesses. She'd been raised outside of the pride by a caring mother, even if she didn't remember it all. Lionesses were taught to be brutal from birth, but Kiera had missed those lessons. It was as if she'd been created and then shaped through the disasters and triumphs of her life to fit him. Not the old him, but the him he was now. And perhaps the same had happened to Beast. Maybe the reason he'd been dragged to the brink was so that he could know his limits and be better for Kiera and the child she carried.

What an ugly puzzle they'd made apart. But oh, what a picture they made together.

She smiled in her sleep, just faintly, and hugged his arm closer. Beast couldn't help the smile on his face. This right here was proof she'd absolutely meant those three words she'd uttered earlier. She even loved him in her sleep when she was completely unconscious. She was still smiling, holding him close. And who would see that little affection? No one but him.

She's it.

Most of the time his lion was made of broken thoughts and death threats, but those two words made all the sense in the world. Kiera was it.

She was good for the monster inside of him. She was a steadying force. She was motivation to make his stand tomorrow. He was picking her, like she'd picked him. Kiera deserved the effort, deserved the protection, deserved every drop of his blood it would take to deliver her into the arms of the Blackwing

Crew.

His animal snarled inside of him, excited by the idea of bloodshed. It had been two years since he'd killed the bachelors. All but the one who got away. All but Justin. Beast had obsessed about this moment. Waited patiently. Kept his body in shape for the fight.

But tonight...

Tonight he was going to take care of Kiera and put off thinking about the meeting. He was going to enjoy his last night when he knew everything was okay.

He was going to make her feel loved because maybe this was all she would have to remember him by.

****

Kiera inhaled deeply and stretched her legs as she eased her bleary eyes open. It was bright here, and her new improved vision was offended by the light beaming through the window of Beast's truck. Whoa, this hotel was fancy as hell. It was all marble columns and valet parking, and a wall of windows that exposed giant chandeliers inside the sprawling entry.

"Are you rich, Beast?" she asked, releasing her

death-grip on his bicep. She didn't miss that his palm covered the swell of her belly

He chuckled a deep, sexy sound. She turned her head fast so she could see the smile that went along with it. His scars had been ugly when she'd thought he got them hurting his pride. Now that she knew better, he had the most handsome face she'd ever laid eyes on.

"Not rich, Kiera, sorry. You'll be a trailer park princess if you stick around for me. I ran a construction team before I came here, though. Did all right and put away some savings."

Honestly, she liked the vision of Beast dressed in a white T-shirt, tattoos and muscles out, hard hat, hole-riddled jeans covered in dust, work gloves, lifting something heavy. Sweating. Subtly, she clamped her legs closed. "That's why you needed the truck? For construction jobs?"

Beast laughed. "Woman, you don't bring a Raptor on construction jobs unless you want to devalue the machine by half in a week, tops. I had an old work truck I brought to the job sites. The Raptor is just for me. I like big trucks, and I like 'em fast."

"You know what they say about men with big

trucks, don't you?" she teased, waggling her eyebrows.

"You better not be about to make a small dick joke."

"Big hands to drive them," she said innocently.

"God," he muttered, shoving his door open. He was smiling, though, and the baby was wiggling in her belly, and everything was perfect.

How could any one person hold this much happiness?

She went to step out of the truck, but Beast was there, so fast he'd blurred to her side, both hands on her hips. Clearly he didn't care about humans seeing what he was. She liked that. She liked that he wouldn't ask her to hide either when she was able to Change again.

His hands were so strong she practically floated down to the ground like a dandelion seed. It was cold out, but she was wearing her thick sweater dress and knee-high boots. Human Kiera would've been freezing and bundled in a jacket, but her new and improved self was perfectly comfortable in the frosty weather.

"Temperature's dropping," Beast said, eyes on

the scenery in front of the hotel. "Can you smell it, Kiera?"

She closed her eyes and inhaled. "All I can smell is you."

A satisfied rumble came from Beast as he pulled her closer. He locked eyes with her for just a moment before he leaned down and pressed his lips to hers. This wasn't urgent, or demanding like earlier. This was another wordless *I love you*. It was a smile against her smile, and a mouth gone soft as he eased back with a sexy smack. Beast whispered, "It's going to snow, Kitty."

Every time he used her pet name in that seductive voice of his, she felt drunk. On numbing legs, she leaned forward when he backed away. He steadied her arms with a laugh that echoed through the parking circle. Eyes sparking with amusement, Beast grabbed their shared duffle bag out of the back seat along with his jacket. Kiera had forgotten hers in the rush to pack this afternoon.

Beast talked to the valet, clapped him on the back in a friendly way, and tipped him a twenty-dollar bill. The valet offered to get him change, but Beast told him, "Nah, keep it."

As Beast pressed his fingertips against the curve of her back and guided her inside, Kiera admitted, "I judge a man on how he treats the people who help him."

Beast frowned down at her. "What do you mean?"

"I like that you just told me you're blue-collar, but in the same minute, you gave a good tip to the valet. When I was a cocktail waitress, I got good at reading people. I could guess what kind of tippers they were by their mannerisms, by how they treated me and the other girls, by how they talked to me. If they were respectful or not, what they acted like when they were tipsy, stuff like that. Sometimes I was wrong, but most of the time I was right. I could call it." She cast a glance up at him and smiled. "You would've surprised me in a good way. You look intimidating, scary even to strangers, and you have a dominant presence, but you're kind when your animal will allow."

"Mmm," he murmured in a very lion-like, deep sound. "I like that you think I'm good."

"I don't think it, I know it. I can see it."

He looked down at her with such an odd

expression of disbelief and hope. Hope? Perhaps hope that she was really telling him the truth and not blowing smoke. She was no smoke-blower, though. Beast was a good man who'd been dealt a bad hand. He'd been thrust into a life that made him make tough decisions and fight for what he wanted.

"Can I help you?" the curvy beauty at the front desk asked. She wore thick-rimmed glasses and sparkly black eyeshadow that made her green eyes look bright and kind as she smiled expectantly at Kiera and Beast.

"Yeah, we're checking in," Beast said as he squared up to the counter and pulled his wallet from his back pocket.

The woman angled her face and frowned, then pointed at Beast. "Do I know you from somewhere?"

"Nope," Beast said immediately, but he was ducking his gaze now. "The room is under Kiera Pierce."

The woman cast a quick, suspicious glance at Kiera, then back to Beast. "You're one of the shifters, aren't you?" She looked around and lowered her voice. "I follow you guys." The woman, Regina, her nametag read, pulled up her phone and started poking buttons and scrolling.

A soft growl rumbled from Beast, but Kiera slid her hand up his back and put on her most polite smile. "We're unregistered to a crew, and we've been driving for a while, had a long night. We really just want to check in and—"

Regina gasped. "Here! I knew it. Beast, dominant mega-psycho. Don't mess with this one unless you want to lose limbs. Badass brawler lion." She grinned excitedly up at Beast. "Lion!" She looked back down at her phone and read faster. "Giant dick." Regina put her hand to her mouth and murmured out the side of her lips, "I believe it," then went back to reading. "Former king, in contention for third under the mother fuckin' dragon, zero STDs, no short-shorts ever, likes to wear monochromatic colors, and is the powerhouse of the Blackwing Trailer Park. Blackwing Trailer Park! You're part of Dark Kane's crew?"

"Where are you reading that from?" Kiera asked, leaning over the counter.

"I'm fangirling so hard right now! Air Ryder Croy posted the Blackwing Crew a couple days ago. Oh! He updated it a couple of hours ago to include you, Kiera Pierce! Lioness, nice. There's a picture of Beast drinking a beer. Your scars are even scarier in person. Can I have your autographs? And one for my little brother. He will *freak* out. He has posters of his favorite predator shifters on his wall."

"Fuckin' Air Ryder," Beast muttered as he signed his name in dark scrawl across the hotel stationary Regina had shoved across the counter to him. He was making the air feel too heavy, too unbreathable, and Kiera's touch wasn't helping.

"I'm never throwing this pen away!" Regina exclaimed. "Brandon!" She waved down a bellhop and started frantically pointing at Beast. "Shifters," she whisper-screamed.

Brandon didn't look like he gave a shit, but he did give them a tired smile as he continued pushing a luggage cart toward the elevator.

Kiera shook her head at the strange turn her life had taken and signed right under Beast's name. He'd ripped through the paper in two places. She pursed her lips against a smile.

Beast scrubbed his hand over his blond hair and pulled a black winter hat on in a gesture that looked more irritation than to keep his head warm. When movement caught her eye, Kiera looked out the massive front windows.

Outside, past the circle drive, fluffy snowflakes were floating to the ground. She gasped. "Beast, you were right! It's snowing."

"Beast is such a cool fucking name. Eeep! I mean freaking." Regina dipped her voice low again. "We're not allowed to say fucking in front of guests, and this is my very first week working here. And I really need this job."

"It's fine. We won't tell," Kiera said with a smile. To Beast, she said, "Can we go out there and enjoy it a minute before we go up to the room?" Really, she needed to get this moody lion outside for a breather before they shoved themselves into a cramped elevator or a small room.

Beast dragged his lightened gaze down her dress to her legs and boots. "You'll get cold."

"No, I won't. I'm warm now."

"What if you get sick?"

"Do lion shifters get sick? You kind of cured me of every possible germ, remember?"

"Right."

He still looked troubled, though, so Kiera snatched his jacket from the crook of his arm and shrugged into it. "Happy?"

"Oh, my gosh!" Regina exclaimed, eyes feverishly bright and trained on the computer she was typing away on.

Beast jumped and asked, "What?"

"You ordered the honeymoon package."

Beast looked at the woman with such exasperation in his eyes Kiera couldn't help but giggle.

"Sorry!" Regina said. "I get so nervous and excitable around you shifters. You're like this badass hot guy, but like a giant, and look at the goosebumps on my arm! You're all scary, but the sexy kind. Oops, I said badass." Regina blew out a shaky breath and said more calmly. "What I mean to say is I can get the welcome platter and sparkling grape juice you ordered if you want to take it outside instead of up to your room. And I can get you a blanket." She gave Kiera the biggest grin. "It'll be so romantic. I'm gonna get you laid, girl."

Kiera was belly laughing now and nodding because that sounded great. "I'm actually really hungry." And if she didn't eat soon, this baby was going to have her good and nauseous again.

"Did we just become friends?" Regina asked.

Kiera cracked up and nodded. "I think we did."

Regina pretended to faint in her chair.

"What is happening right now?" Beast asked, his eyes narrowed on the limp woman.

"I think she is going to set up a picnic in the snow for us," Kiera explained.

"Yes!" Regina said, coming back to life. "Be right back. I'll get you the good stuff. Are you sure you don't want champagne?"

Kiera cupped her belly and shook her head. "Grape juice sounds good to me."

"Right." Regina bustled off, then brought a platter of chocolate covered strawberries, green and purple grapes, and assorted cheeses with crackers. She handed the unopened bottle of sparkling juice and a dark green comforter over the counter as well. "Don't tell my boss. He's a total snobby prick." She poked her nose up like a pig and winked at Kiera.

"We're very good at keeping secrets," Kiera told her.

"I bet you are, you saucy shifters." She was giving Beast the hungry eyes, and Kiera was pretty sure Regina would've fit right into the D-Team.

Beast paid, then had Brandon take their things up to the room. When he looked at the keycard for the room number, Beast hesitated. He huffed a breath and gave Kiera the strangest look. "This number just keeps showing up."

"What number?"

"Ten-ten."

Chills washed over her forearms. "Hey, I'm staying in room ten-ten at the motel outside of Bryson City."

"I know. It's also the number on Kane's house. And it's one of the numbers Dustin makes all of his wishes on. Anytime I'm around him at 10:10, or 11:11, he loudly makes ridiculous wishes."

"Ridiculous wishes?" she asked as she followed Beast out the sliding front doors.

"Yeah, he told me all his wishes came true the day he paired up with Emma, so now he makes all these dumb wishes for me." He muttered as an aside, "It's fucking annoying."

"What wishes?" she asked as they jogged across the street toward a garden lot with grassy hills, mums all over the landscaping, and a quaint pond in the center.

Beast sighed, which tapered into a snarl. He was holding all the supplies, but he still rested his fingertips under her elbow to keep her from slipping on the ice patches forming on the road. "First one I heard was 'I wish Beast would realize he is my best friend.' He does that shit to piss me off."

Kiera snorted. She believed him. Dustin had a fascination with irking people. "What else?"

"Wish number two that I heard… And by the way, he looks so dumb when he does it. He puts his finger on his watch, tilts his head to the sky, closes his eyes, and says them with such earnest and a stupid smile on his face because he knows I'm glaring at him. Wish number two, he wished I would share my teriyaki beef jerky with him two Thursdays ago."

Kiera's smile stretched so big. She put her hand out and caught snowflakes on her palm. "What was wish number three?"

"He did that one after we saw you for the first time at the barbecue place. He wished for me to get a blow job and be nicer to everyone. Number four was 'I wish Beast would smile more.' Number five was 'I wish Beast would go camping with me.' Fucking *camping*, Kiera. We live in a trailer park, and he wants to go camping out in the woods right next to his damn house like a boy scout. Number six. 'I wish Beast would forgive me for drinking all his moonshine.' Seven. 'I wish Beast would stop choking me.' And last but not least, eight. 'I wish Beast would stop being a double-douche-biscuit and pick Kiera.'"

Kiera wrapped her arms around his bicep and rested her cheek on the curve of his shoulder. "So wishing on 10:10 does work then."

Beast kissed the top of her head. "I guess sometimes it does. I'm still not going camping with him, though. And I probably won't stop choking him anytime soon. Asshole drives me insane."

"What else do you like to do?" she asked, her boots echoing against the concrete of the sidewalk that wound around the pond.

"I do weapons training. I shoot guns when the fury in me gets too much. Anytime I wanted to jump the gun on challenging Justin, I would go to the range, or out to the middle of nowhere, and unload all that stress with shooting targets. Long range. I like rifles. I like the precision, the guns, cleaning, the scopes, sighting them in, everything. Everything about it calms me and focuses my energy on something other than obsessing over Justin. What do you like to do?"

"I knit scarves."

Beast laughed a rich, echoing sound. "I shoot and keep my body in shape to fight, and you knit scarves."

Kiera pushed him playfully. "Shut your sexy mouth. You're being mean. And knitting scarves isn't the only thing I like to do. You just didn't let me finish."

"Okay, I'm ready. Tell me what other badass stuff you like to do."

"I can cook. I'm really good at cooking tenderloin. And breakfast food. And sometimes when I get upset, or have my own stuff to work through, I bake…and clean." Kiera frowned. "And none of this is as cool as weapons training."

Beast chuckled and shook his head. "If you teach me how to make biscuits and gravy, I will teach you to shoot."

"That's the easiest thing to make in the world."

"Oh, my gosh," he said, giving her an exasperated look. "Are you negotiating backwards?"

"Right. Nope. I'll teach you the ins and outs of sausage gravy, and you take me to the range. And also teach me how to…how did you say it? Brawl like a gorilla?"

Beast's grin curved even wider. "You're making me really hard right now, just so you know."

Kiera squeaked and looked down, and sure enough, he was sporting one serious boner.

"Good."

"Feeling cocky about yourself now, are you?" he asked, spreading out the blanket on the snow-speckled grass.

"Yep."

"Come here," he growled, pulling her down onto the blanket beside him.

She giggled and laid on her back, looking up at the churning gray clouds as fluffy white flakes floated this way and that around them. She stuck her tongue out until she caught one. Beast laughed. He was on his side, elbow on the blanket, palm under his cheek as he watched her with dancing eyes.

And then he did the most incredible thing anyone had ever done in her life. He leaned in and kissed her lips gently, and then just as tenderly, he moved down and kissed the swell of her belly, too.

His face went serious as he rested his cheek against the taut curve of her stomach. "Tonight while you were sleeping in the truck, I made a wish."

"On 10:10?"

He nodded, draped his arm over her hips, and cradled her close. His other hand slid up her stomach to cup the growing life there. "I wished I could keep you both."

"Beast," she whispered, sliding her hand down to his cheek. The rasp of his whiskers felt good against her palm. "Wishes work on 10:10," she said, feeling desperate to ease the sadness that had suddenly flooded his eyes.

He smiled back at her, so strikingly handsome with the pond behind him and the white snow floating all around. He covered her stomach protectively. "Yeah. Sometimes they do."

FOURTEEN

Kiera stretched her hand out for Beast, but though his side of the bed was warm, it was empty. She blinked blearily at the soft gray light that filtered through the opening between the blackout curtains. Propping up on her elbow, she frowned at Beast's back. Every muscle was tense, and he was sitting on the edge of the mattress with his head in his hands. Kiera crawled to him and laid her hand on his back. He was vibrating with power. She could feel it pulsing through her and bouncing off her bones. The air was so heavy it was like trying to breath cement.

"What's wrong?" she choked out, sliding her palm gently up his spine.

"Bad dream, Kiera." Beast's voice came out a

terrifying, gravelly sound that belonged to demons. "Go back to sleep, I'm okay."

"Tell me about it so it won't come true." Those words tugged at something deep in her memory though. While she waited for Beast to summon the strength to tell her, she dug deep at the sense of déjà vu. And suddenly, like lightning, the memory flashed across her mind. Kiera gasped. "I just remembered something about my mom," she huffed on a stunned breath. "Something that was buried."

Beast twisted and looked at her over his shoulder. His eyes couldn't pass for human, glowed bright gold, and his face had half morphed into his ferocious animal. "What is it?" His teeth were still gritted, jaw clenched, body rigid as stone, but his eyes softened a little.

"I used to get nightmares when I was a kid. Bad ones. I would get them for a few weeks, every night, and then nothing for months, and then three weeks on again, a few months off. My mom knew the pattern, so she would sleep in my room when I was going through it. And every time I woke up scared, she would say, 'Tell me about it so it won't come true.'" Kiera smiled and rested her cheek on the back of his neck, wrapped her arms around his strong middle. "I don't know if it really works, but I believed it did, and none of them ever came true. If I said them out loud, they couldn't hurt me anymore." She laid a light peck on his shoulder and squeezed him gently. "So tell me, Beast, and that way it won't come true." She dipped her voice to a whisper. "I'll help you carry the dream to the cliffs, and then we'll throw it over together."

Beast huffed a breath, then another, and finally the air became thinner and easier to breath. He slid his hand over hers, as if he wanted to keep her against him just like this. He rolled his head back and rested it on the top of hers. "I was with my pride. We were hunting. We had woods where we lived, but these looked different. More pines than oaks. It was cold. December, maybe. Stormy but not snowing. Gray sky, and pine needles quieting our footsteps. The woods even smelled different. I looked to my left and right, and they were there. Alisha was right beside me, mouth open, panting like we'd been traveling a long way already. She and the others were waiting for my signal. I thought they were on the trail of something. A deer if we were lucky. Hunting deer always brought us closer. I was confused because I couldn't smell any deer. I smelled something else."

"What was it?" she murmured.

"You."

Kiera stopped stroking his chest.

"We were hunting you. You stood at the edge of this clearing, a steep cliff jutting up behind you, trapping you. You looked beautiful, hair whipping in the wind. You weren't crying. You looked me dead in the eyes with such hatred. I was proud and heartbroken, all at once. You wore this flowing green dress that fluttered against your figure. Your eyes were gold, and beside you stood a little boy. Three maybe. Looked like you, same blue eyes. He looked scared, and he was clinging to your leg. I turned to lay into my pride for what they were doing. I was going to punish them severely for hunting you and your child. I knew it had to be jealousy because I'd *chosen* you, and they were just pride females. But when I looked at Alisha, it wasn't her. None of the lionesses were mine. I didn't recognize a single one, and when I looked down at my paws, they were different from mine. Different size, different scars, different color. My mane was black."

"Justin," Kiera whispered in horror.

"Yeah. I was leading the Tarian Pride in a hunt for you and your cub. And Kiera, it felt so *real*," he rumbled. "You won't be coming with me today."

"But Beast, this is my battle."

"A battle you can't protect yourself from. Not while you're pregnant, not while you can't call on your animal."

"I can't ask you to do this alone."

"And you didn't," he said, turning suddenly. His bright gold eyes pleaded for understanding. "I don't want you anywhere around Justin or his pride. Not today, not ever. If something happens, you take my truck, and you drive straight back to Kane's Mountains. You plead sanctuary, you register both you and your unborn cub to the Blackwings—"

"Beast stop! We're going to do this together. Stop talking like this."

"Kiera, listen. Listen!" When he gripped the back of her neck, her lioness drew up inside of her, wanted to expose her neck in submission. She could see it there in his eyes, the rigidity he'd ruled his pride with. He had never pushed her to obey him before, but on this, he wasn't going to budge. She could see that much in the grim set to his mouth. "I'm not saying I'm not going to come back for you. I'm saying if I *can't*, don't ever give Justin an opening to get to you."

Beast was conjuring something deep inside of her, opening her lioness up with the way he was looking at her. His nostrils flared slightly, and his gaze raked down her sleep shirt to her thighs, then with a slow blink, he lifted that brilliant gaze back to hers, his pupils adjusting slightly as he focused on her.

"Sexy mate," she whispered, running her hand up his chest.

"Again," he growled, pulling her hand until it went over his shoulder.

"Sexy mate," she repeated breathlessly. God, she would do anything he told her to right now.

He bit the inside of her bicep almost hard enough to break skin, and then he crawled up her body, maneuvering her toward the middle of the bed, his lips inches from hers. "Turn over."

This was the part she'd hated with Justin, but with Beast, her big, dominant man wouldn't hurt her. She trusted him, and right now, her inner lioness was more present than she'd been since Apex stole her away. Kiera was flushed with need. She pushed up and kissed him, pushed her tongue past his lips and then sucked hard on his bottom lip. She even let off a warning growl. *Be gentle.* When she released his lip, Beast smiled in that wicked way of his, and he looked so damn proud of her.

Warmth pooled in Kiera's middle as she slowly turned over onto her hands and knees. She thought he would pull the lion breeding shit immediately, but Beast had other plans. He squeezed her ass firmly, then ran his hand up her back. Kiera's instinct kicked in, and she bowed her spine like her happy lioness urged. He leaned over her, one arm locked beside hers, the other petting up and down her back, massaging her, kneading her, setting her on fire, cell by cell. He ran kisses along her shoulder blades, one to the other, biting, sucking, rasping against her sensitive skin with his three-day beard. Kiera was already purring, rocking back and forth slowly, tempting him, tempting herself. She could feel the swollen head of his cock if she rocked back far enough, right where she needed him.

Beast used his knee to spread hers wider, and

before she was even settled, he slid into her from behind, stretching her as he grunted and rested his forehead between her shoulder blades. This wasn't the primal, painful bucking it had been with Justin. This was slow and steady, moving together, his fingers intertwined with hers as he warmed her back with his torso. He grasped her other hand and pulled it between her legs. She could feel him there, moving within her. His kisses were still soft on her shoulder, but he was ending them with a teasing bite every time he pushed all the way into her.

She'd never been able to come like this, but Beast was working her toward release at a shocking rate. Every stroke brought such an intense wave of pleasure, she moaned at each peak, just before he eased back and pushed into her again, building more and more pressure until she was blind with how good he was making her feel. He pressed her hand harder between her legs and clamped his teeth on her shoulder, then released her.

"Fuck, Kiera, I'm close."

She didn't have time to say, "Me, too," before the first pulse of her orgasm clenched around him.

"Beast, Beast, Beast," she whispered helplessly as

he reacted.

Beast reared back and slammed into her, faster and faster, his hand gripping hers hard, his torso flexing against her back as he moved.

A snarl ripped through him as he thrust into her hard, his teeth rough on her back. He released her skin and slammed into her again, his release throbbing right along with hers. He didn't roll off and leave her cold, no. Beast rocked with her until he'd dragged every aftershock from her. It was like he didn't want to lose this connection, and she got it. She didn't want to think this might be their last time together, but she didn't know what would happen today.

It felt as if her life was on this runaway train that was unstoppable now, and there was this terrifying possibility that they wouldn't survive the crash. She hated the uncertainty.

"Shhh." Beast positioned her to her side and lay behind her, curled his big, strong body around hers and pulled the blanket over their hips.

Kiera swallowed the growl she didn't realize she was making and, muscle-by-muscle relaxed into the strength of her mate. His arms were so powerful around her, his body so hard against her back. He lifted her hair up to fan the pillow and buried his face against the back of her neck. With a sigh, he murmured against her skin, "I love you, Kiera."

Kiera gritted her teeth and glared at the wall because that was it. That was his just-in-case goodbye. That was him telling her the thing she needed to hear before he left her here to hope and pray he wouldn't bleed out under the jaws of the monster who had clawed up his face and taken his pride.

Well, fuck his goodbyes.

She didn't know how she was going to do it, but she was going to that meeting. Beast had weeded out the Blackwings' help, and now hers, too, turning himself into a one-man wrecking crew against an entire pride. Screw that. That's not how mates worked. That's not how lions hunted.

This wasn't just his battle, and she wasn't going to live with what-ifs on the chance her badass Beast didn't take down the Tarian Pride.

She'd been a rogue all her life, but this is where the winds changed. This was where the breeze became the hurricane.

She picked.

She picked him, picked motherhood, picked the crew, picked Kane's Mountains, picked happiness.

Kiera. Picked. This. Life.

This was the beginning of their story, not tapering toward their end. Fuck endings and fuck Justin for drawing just-in-case goodbyes from Beast's lips.

She was finally, *finally* ready to put down roots, but it was no life without Beast, who had showed her so much about herself already. He steadied her and made her feel invincible. He made her feel like everything was going to be okay, and it had been a long damn time since she'd hosted those thoughts. She'd got a taste of good, and she wasn't going back.

She needed Beast.

And even if he didn't realize it yet, he needed her, too.

FIFTEEN

Kiera wrapped her arms around her stomach and drew her knees up to her chest as she leaned back against the wall, right by the toilet. She glared at the porcelain. She hadn't gotten sick, just felt like she could. This is the part of pregnancy she didn't enjoy.

"Kiera?" Beast rumbled, knocking softly.

"I'm okay," she said shakily. She still felt light-headed and weak, but that would pass soon. It always did.

The door creaked open, and Beast peeked in with a worried frown marring his face. "The baby is still making you sick?" He came to kneel in front of her and pushed her hair out of her face, then lifted her chin and checked her eyes. For what, she didn't know.

"I looked it up. Morning sickness is supposed to be over at three months...right?"

Kiera laughed weakly. "Everyone is different. Some people have it their whole pregnancy. And the term morning sickness is also bullshit. It can happen at any time in the day."

Beast scooted closer between her spread legs. "How do I fix you?"

God, he was so cute. He was this muscled-up, scar-faced titan, and she'd never seen a more worried look on anyone's face in her entire life.

"I think I need something to eat. I have some crackers in my purse."

"Crackers? No." He shook his head like he was offended. "You need pancakes and bacon and steak and waffles and anything you and the baby want."

Kiera leaned forward and rested her forehead against his chest. His heartbeat was pounding. "I'm not going to die from this, Beast. The crackers will help until I can get a bigger meal."

Beast bolted away so fast she almost face planted between her own knees. The man blurred—blurred!—into the other room and was back in seconds, ripping into the package of saltines with his teeth like an animal. He shoved three at her, turned, and strode toward the door, hesitated, then jogged back to her and placed the entire package into her hands. "Water," he murmured. "You need water."

Kiera watched in amusement as he rushed to the sink and filled a glass. "Ice?" he asked in a panicked voice.

"No, plain is fine."

"Shit," he breathed as he handed her the glass. He backed up a few paces and stared down at her with wide eyes, his hands on his hips. "I feel like I need to…I need to…"

"There's a pancake house a couple doors down. Waffles sound good."

"I'm gonna do that. I'm gonna get you more food. Don't move. Or move if you want. I'll be back. Do you need a blanket?" He shook his head hard. "You look really pretty, even when you are pale and sick."

Kiera giggled. "I love you, ya big old worried brute. Extra butter and syrup."

"Right," he said, shoving his wallet into the back pocket of his jeans. It dragged the waist of his pants down enough for her to see the lowest two abs of his eight-pack.

"Uuum," he said before he left, looking around and patting his pockets like the thought he forgot something. "I'll be back. Extra butter and syrup," he murmured as he strode out the door.

Well, he'd sure distracted her off her nausea. She stood carefully. Both key cards were still sitting on the counter, which meant she was definitely going to have to let Beast back in when he returned. At least he'd given her the perfect opportunity to call for reinforcements.

Kiera pulled her phone out of her back pocket and texted Dustin, who had programmed the entire D-Team's phone numbers into her phone at some point with nicknames for them all.

Big Dick Dustin.

Emma Perfect Titties.

Anal Gland, which she guessed was Logan.

Winter the Splinter.

Best Friend Werepussy. That one was apparently Beast.

She texted Big Dick Dustin because he always seemed down for a bad idea.

Beast is pushing me out of the meeting. I think he

needs backup. Send.

The reply was almost immediate. *No shit. We're at the coffee shop across the street.*

Kiera frowned. *Wait, what? Beast told you to stay home.* Send.

Hey remember that time Beast was the alpha of the Blackwing Crew?

No. Send.

Me either, doll-face. That's why I didn't listen. We camped out in the damn parking lot all night. I got a blow job. My neck is stiff from sleeping in the car though. I said stiff. Oh look, there's Beast. Why is he running? Emma says hi.

Kiera blinked hard. Where did she even start on her response to that. *Tell Emma I say hi back. Congrats on the BJ. I'm glad you didn't listen because I think Beast is in trouble. He's running to the pancake place a couple doors down to grab me some breakfast.* Send.

There is protein in semen. You coulda had breakfast already.

Dustin. Focus. Send.

A couple minutes passed before the response buzzed her phone. *How much trouble?*

Bring in the crew and more kind of trouble. I have a bad feeling. Send.

Already done. I'll light a fire under them to get here faster.

A wave of relief flooded through her. Dustin was all A-Team today.

Kiera began readying for the day, but she didn't even have her hair completely fixed by the time a knock sounded at the door. Kiera smiled. Beast had probably sprinted to the café and bullied the staff to rush an order. It was so funny watching him worry so deeply over a little morning sickness.

There was another knock. "I'm coming," she said with a giggle. Panicking alpha lion.

Kiera set her phone on the counter and pulled open the door. She gasped and startled hard before trying to shove the door closed as fast as she could. Justin slammed his hand on the edge of the door and shoved it open again. His hand was over her mouth before she could get a single screech out, but she wasn't human anymore. She shoved him back and bolted into the bathroom. She slammed the door so fast she almost severed his fingertips. Desperately, she shoved her weight against the barrier and texted

Dustin.

He—

The door rocketed inward, and it was all she could do to send that much. The first two letters of *help*, and dear Lord let Dustin understand the SOS. With the force of Justin's entry, she skidded across the tile and banked off the wall, all while protecting her belly.

Justin was just as terrifying as she remembered. Green eyes turned a muddy gold, black hair, full lips, perfect nose, flawless, empty smile, cleanly shaven, and tall as the freaking doorway. Beautiful man with the devil in his soul.

"The girl at the front desk announced your location to the world, Kiera. You got sloppy." His hand was tangled in the back of her hair, other hand over her mouth again. "Miss me, bitch?"

"Let go of me," she yelled behind his hand. She struggled, but she didn't want the baby hurt.

Justin smelled like arousal, which brought the nausea back. He cupped her belly with his giant hand and yanked her mouth to his so hard their teeth knocked. She screamed into his mouth and pushed, but Justin had adjusted to her new strength and wasn't holding back now. Furious, Kiera bit his lip.

Justin grunted and yanked out of her bite, but the damage was done. Blood streamed down his chin.

She spat in his face. "I belong to Beast now."

Justin ripped her sweater to the side to expose the mangled layers of claiming marks. Rage built in his gaze as he dragged it back to hers. "The fuck you are. My cub. My claim. You'll come quietly, or I'll end you both right in this fucking hotel room."

He would do it, too. His voice rang with such conviction she knew he would hurt her beyond repair. And it wasn't just her at risk. If she didn't survive, her baby didn't either.

A man in his forties with a thick gray beard appeared in the doorway. "We have to hurry." He was built like a brick house, and his eyes were glowing lion gold. What the hell was happening? She'd expected the Tarian lionesses at the meeting. Not other male lion shifters.

Justin dragged her by the hair out into the hallway, hand over her damn mouth again, tempting her to sever it completely. The baby, though. The baby.

The hallway was lined with six men, all reeking

of dominance, all with those tell-tale gold eyes that said something awful was happening.

"Kiera, meet the council."

Oh. Shit.

A couple of them were smiling cruelly, but most of them watched her with dead eyes, or hatred in them, as Justin dragged her past. Justin hadn't brought his pride of females to hunt her. He'd brought the damn council. These men were law, and they were allowing this. Helping even.

Angry tears burned her eyes, but she blinked hard to keep them to herself. Justin and this council of assholes didn't deserve to see her emotions.

Her phone was lying on the floor of the bathroom, Beast was getting breakfast, and clearly, Dustin hadn't seen these men roll up because he would've been here. She tried to stall, but Justin pushed her faster and shoved her through a door that led to an emergency stairwell. She had no control down the flight of steps because Justin was dragging her, and the silver-bearded council member was now helping him. Fucking lions.

"You've been so good at hiding, Kiera," Justin gritted out low. "So good. I've been obsessed with finding you before the baby is born. None of my females pull this shit, and maybe that's why my lion is so damn interested in keeping you. Or maybe it's the baby, and fuck you after you have it. I haven't decided yet, but you'll be registered to me by tomorrow. Stupid bitch thought you could register to a crew. Seriously? You're a lion now, clearly. I can smell you. Fur and dominance, and listen to that gorgeous snarl in your throat. My claiming mark worked. I gave you your lion back, and this is how you repay me? By taking my cub," he yelled into her ear.

Kiera hunched her shoulders in pain. She still wasn't used to the sensitive hearing. Justin shoved her out of the emergency exit. The alarm blared but he and the council didn't seem to care. A mud-brown Yukon sat waiting for them. The man in the front seat looked as grim as the others. All the doors on this side were open, but she wouldn't get in there. Kiera buckled her legs and struggled against Justin's hold. His hand went so tight in her hair she thought he would rip it out. When he got too rough, Kiera screamed against his hand as loud and long as she could. He barked out, "Stop it!" and jerked her head to the side painfully.

As she locked her legs against the sides of the door, she bit him on the meat of the hand. There was yelling, and suddenly, something hard knocked against the side of her skull. She was stunned with the blinding pain, and the world blurred around her. She fought still, but she didn't have very good control of her limbs. Not when her ears were ringing like this. Warmth trickled down the side of her face and got in her eye.

Mindlessly, she murmured, "Beast," but there was no way he could hear her terrified whisper.

Justin and the others muscled her into the SUV. When she sat sandwiched and limp between the alpha of the Tarian Pride and the silver-bearded council member, she knew it was over.

She'd been naïve to think Justin would have a rational conversation in the meeting Dustin had set up. Beast would've, but he was a good man. As she lifted her bleary gaze to Justin, who was licking her blood off the ring on his right hand, it was all so clear. Beast had never been the monster everyone thought he'd been. Justin was.

Now and for always, she would be registered as his pride, his female, his property. He would break her slowly and discard her as soon as she gave him a cub.

As buckled her seatbelt, and watched the city blurring by out the window, her heart broke.

For a blinding moment, she'd had hope that everything would be okay. She'd held happiness in her hand. *In her hand.* It had been in her grasp, and it had been so beautiful.

But she'd just lost the war for her freedom before it even started.

SIXTEEN

Beast smiled at the little baby onesie in the glass display case. It was green and said *Momma's lil Waffle Maker* on it. It was so damn cute he had to swallow a purr. Subtly, Beast looked around to make sure no one had been watching the dumb smile stretch across his face. Good thing the D-Team wasn't here. They would rib him relentlessly if they knew how badly he was falling apart just thinking about watching Kiera's pregnancy, watching her belly grow, feeling the baby, taking care of them...holding it.

He hoped it was a girl. No, a boy. No...a girl. Gah, he didn't care either way.

He would do anything for his mate and her child. *Anything*.

Over the past day, he'd had bouts of insecurity about his ability to keep them safe, but that was done now. He was coming back to them no matter what. The draw was too big. Kiera was offering him this perfect life he'd always dreamed about but that had always stayed just out of reach.

She could fix him, and in return, he would keep her safe for always. Beast would be damned if he let Justin or his pride mess with what he and Kiera were building.

His phone buzzed in his pocket.

The to-go waitress at Wally-Pancakes leaned out of the kitchen and told him, "I'll have it out for you in two minutes."

"Thanks," he murmured, wishing it was ready now. He'd hated seeing Kiera ill. He wanted to take care of her, and all of his instincts were screaming to go back to her now.

His phone buzzed again. It was a call, not a text, so he pulled it out. *Worst Friend* flashed across the caller ID. Mother fucker. "What, Dustin?" he answered.

"I think you lost something, Beasty Boy." The sound of Dustin's car engine was loud in the phone, and he could hear him shifting gears. Emma sounded frantic in the background, directing Dustin where to go.

"What are you talking about?"

"Justin has Kiera!"

Dread froze Beast into an immovable statue. "What the fuck are you talking about?"

"They came for her the second you left, Beast. Now get in your truck and haul ass. No one is ready yet, and I can't do this alone. We're on I-40 headed away from Bryson City. I'm giving you to Emma so I can drive. Beast...*move*."

"Shit," Beast blurted, forcing his body to react. He bolted for the door and didn't even try to hide his speed as he sprinted to the hotel parking lot.

No time to wait on the tired looking valet, Beast muscled past him and yanked the key compartment open, scanned for his key, grabbed it, and bolted for the parking lot behind the hotel. He made black tire marks peeling out, and barely stopped to check traffic before he was heading for the highway.

Dustin and Emma were here. Kiera was kidnapped? Justin better not lay a finger on her. Fuck, Beast was going to gut him.

He jammed the speaker button on his phone and shoved it in a cup holder. He could hear Emma directing Dustin in a muffled voice over the phone. Beast's Raptor was built to move, and thank God for that blessing right now because he needed all the speed he could get to catch up with Kiera. The engine roared when he asked his ride for more as he jerked it around a puttering car in the slow lane. No cops, no cops, no cops right now!

Cars honked as he blazed by, but fuck it, they didn't know. His whole world was in danger.

"Beast!" Emma yelled on the speaker phone. "Are you still there?"

"I'm here. Where are you?"

She spouted off the exit sign they were passing. Ten miles ahead. "We're hitting more traffic and a little bit of ice, so we're slowing down a little with dodging. Beast, there's a mountain range ahead. We're gonna cut right through it. This is where it needs to go down."

Oh, he got it. They needed to stop Justin in the woods and hope for less human eyes on them.

"Beast, what do you want us to do?" Emma asked. "We're right on them, but traffic is making it hard to stick close."

"Shit, shit, shit. What exit now?"

Emma told him. Eight miles ahead. Beast was panicked. He had no control over any of this.

"Beast," Dustin growled into the phone. "If they get away, we won't be getting her back, do you understand? They've got eight men and her."

"Eight?" Eight men. Eight men. Fuck, what did that mean? Justin didn't have his pride. Were they bachelors? No way. Bachelor lions wouldn't have anything to do with Justin after he took over a pride. He was *other* to them now. He wouldn't be able to control them. So where the fuck did he get this kind of muscle?

"Yeah, they have a full frickin' Yukon, man," Dustin said. "Gold eyes, all of them."

It hit him like an avalanche. Beast couldn't help the roar that bellowed from him. He slammed his fist against the steering wheel. Justin brought in the fucking council. Dustin was right. If they got away, Beast would never get her back again. Not if the council was backing this kidnapping. It would be him versus the entirety of the lion shifter race to get her back.

"Clip them," he ground out.

"I'm sorry, *clip them*?" Dustin enunciated carefully over the noise of him shifting gears. "Beast, this is my car. My baby."

"This is Kiera, Dustin! My mate. My cub. Blackwing through and through. We're crew, now fucking clip them. Stop them in the mountains. Don't get out of the car after. I'll take care of it."

"Tighten your seatbelt," Dustin growled in a muffled voice.

"What are you doing?" Emma asked over the roar of the engine.

"Beast, before I fuck up my car, you have to say it."

Beast growled.

"Say it!" Dustin yelled.

"Aw fuck, Dustin! You're my best friend!"

The line went dead, and Beast's heart leapt into his throat. *God, let them all be okay. Let Kiera be wearing a seatbelt. Let the Yukon stay on all four wheels. Let them not roll. Let Dustin and Emma keep control. Let me get there in time.*

The road had gone down to two lanes surrounded by woods. Traffic was too thick here, so he zoomed off road and blasted up the side, spewing dirt and rocks and plumes of dust behind him. Too close to the trees, he pulled onto the shoulder, and just in time for the road to drop off the side. Ahead, the brake lights were flashing and people were slowing down. Smoke billowed up ahead.

Please God, let them be okay.

So close.

Beast maneuvered over both lanes and onto the other shoulder of the mountainside. It was such a tight fit against a cliff wall, his side view mirror got scraped off, but screw it. All he could think about was Kiera, the baby, and his crew.

And then Emma was there in the middle of the road, ushering traffic to the side, creating a lane for him. She looked terrified, and her nose was bleeding. She waved frantically for him.

Beast rolled down his window and slowed.

Emma tumbled over her words in a rush. "They're all alive, ran into the woods with her. Beast! Dustin went after them!"

Fuck. "I'll take care of him!" he yelled as he gassed it toward the wreck.

Dustin had rolled his car, but the Yukon was

upright, slammed into a tree, thick gray smoke billowing from under the smashed hood. The windows were cracked, but not broken. No one had been ejected.

Beast slammed on the brakes and skidded to a stop, left the car on and ripped out of his seatbelt. And then he was running. He could smell them. The scent of dominant, brawler, male lions saturated every molecule.

A long howl sounded. It was the cry of a lone wolf on the hunt. *Ease off, Dustin.*

Beast ripped off his shirt and kicked out of his shoes as he sprinted through the snowy woods. The buckle of his belt sounded as he ducked a low hanging limb, and with a few clumsy steps, he was free of his pants, too. He could smell Kiera now, and that spurred the urge to Change. Beast sprinted, leapt, and as he sailed through the air, his lion shredded him instantly on the way down. He landed on all four paws but didn't slow in the new body. He could hear them now. Another howl. *Back the fuck off, Dustin!* Pushing the lions would get the wolf killed, and Emma needed her mate.

The challenging roar of a lion sounded long and

loud, tapered, then started up again. Beast knew that sound. It was the same challenge that had filled his heart with hatred for the past two years. It was Justin's voice that taunted him. He'd taken everything from him, and Beast would be damned if he did it again.

Justin had signed his ticket to hell the second he'd touched Kiera.

Beast threw his head back and bellowed his response.

Challenge accepted.

SEVENTEEN

Kiera's neck hurt, and her head was throbbing. The air was too cold, and the woods too fragrant. Justin's grip was too tight on her arm, and she snarled at him as he pushed her toward a cliff face that jutted straight up. Dumbass had gotten himself cornered. She would've laughed if she wasn't in so much danger.

Justin jammed his finger at Kiera. "Watch her." She wanted to rip his throat out.

"You can't lose this, or it sets a bad precedence," Silver Beard murmured.

"I fucking know, Lucian! Why do you think I tried to avoid this? I can feel him coming for her." Justin gripped the back of his neck and paced. He was red-faced with blazing eyes, and a vein throbbed at his temple. He looked insane.

"You should be scared," she murmured.

"Of who, bitch? Huh?" he yelled. "Of Beast? Tell me, how do you stomach fucking him when his face is disfigured because of me. I've beat him once—"

"With an entire group of bachelors, you overconfident asshole!"

"What is she talking about?" Lucian asked, his gold eyes narrowed suspiciously.

"Nothing. I challenged Beast, he lost, and obviously he's lying to this stupid bitch about what really happened."

Oooh, so the council was unaware that Justin was involved in the murder of Beast's pride. She couldn't have been the only one to catch all the false notes in Justin's voice as he'd spewed excuses.

"If she joins the Blackwing Crew, what do you think will happen to any female unhappy with pride life?" one of the other council members asked. He was removing his shirt. "They'll be flooding away from prides to join crews! Our entire species will be tainted. Our entire way of life will be destroyed." The man spat near Kiera's feet. "Rogue just like your mother. Trouble just like her."

"He won't take her from me," Justin snarled, kicking out of his shoes.

It was snowing again in big flurries, and the wind was frigid, but that wasn't the reason for the gooseflesh on Kiera's arms. It was the long, lone wolf howl that filled the air. She rested her back against the rock face and cradled her belly protectively.

"Kill the wolf," Lucian ordered a pair of the council-members. The jacked-up behemoths Changed into massive lions and side-by-side trotted off toward the tree line.

"Run, Dustin!" she screamed.

Justin was on her so fast it stole her breath away. He was in her face, fist raised, eyes wild. He didn't blast her, though. Her cowering against the rock seemed to pacify him. Justin liked having that kind of control. He huffed an empty laugh. She hated everything about him.

"You'll want me again after this," he promised her, stripping off his shirt. "I remember the old you, Kiera. The desperate one. The one who needed the bite. The one who liked to be fucked. It was so fucking beautiful how badly you needed me. You'll feel that again when he is dead. I promise. I'll bond your lion to me if it takes me your entire life, however short or long that may be." He snarled up his lip and gave her his back as if she was no threat at all. And he was right. She couldn't call her lion and keep the pregnancy, so she was stuck. This was the worst feeling in the world, being trapped with monsters. The real kind.

Justin's lion was hideous. Oh, she'd heard his pride talk about him, so proud to have a striking male like him. Cream colored fur, a black mane, and muscular anatomy. His battle scars were light, like thin silver spider webs on his body. Perhaps she was biased. Maybe Kiera just knew what he looked like on the inside, and therefore it tainted his outsides to her.

He arched his neck back and roared.

With a gasp, Kiera covered her ears. And almost immediately, his challenge was answered with a roar that was so terrifyingly loud it chilled her blood.

When she saw Beast, a slow, proud smile stretched her lips. He came out of the trees unrushed, gait graceful, eyes on Justin, then to her, then back to Justin. The side of his scarred lip curled up, exposing the longest canines she'd ever seen. Justin was big for a lion, but Beast was *beast*. He had fifty pounds of muscle on his rival, at least. His chestnut colored mane was full, and his ears were flattened. His eyes flashed with the promise of death.

Even from here, in her human form, she could feel Beast's fury. It was like a mountain on her shoulders and poison in her lungs. She could almost taste his rage on the air currents.

"Ooooh, he's gonna kill youuu," she sang softly. "Bye, Justin."

Justin flashed her a hate-filled glance over his shoulder, but she was ready for him with two middle fingers and a smile.

Justin kicked into a trot, and across the field, Beast did the same, two titans on a collision course. There would only be one survivor in this challenge. There was too much bad blood, too many evil deeds done, too much hatred for Beast to let him live.

Lucian bumped her shoulder, but she winced away. "What did you mean about the bachelors?"

"You backed the last of the monsters that killed Beast's pride, Lucian. Poor choice."

The lions were running now, kicking up snow behind them as they charged, tails up. There was no hesitation or circling. There was no sizing each other up first. They clashed with the force of an earthquake and went immediately to war in a frenzy of violence that made her want to look away but made it impossible to give her attention to anything else. Beast was in control from minute one with his long-reach clawing and piercing teeth. Snarling and the echo of resounding slaps filled the clearing. They locked up, and Justin was slammed to the ground. Crimson stained Justin's leg, and when he spun away, she caught a glimpse of his ruined face. Beast had gotten his teeth into his muzzle. Justin hunched defensively, but Beast was back on him in an instant. They were attached by teeth, ripping and piercing, spinning and rolling. The snow was making it harder to see, and around her, the council-members were Changing.

"What are you doing?" she asked, panicking.

"Doesn't matter who we backed," Lucian murmured hollowly. "We can't lose a pregnant lioness to the dragons. Can't lose you to a crew. Can't have a lion cub registered to the Blackwings. All you had to do was stick with the pride." He gave her a dead-eyed look. "Beast's death is on you."

She didn't understand. In the clearing, Beast had his jaws locked onto Justin's throat, and the black-maned lion wasn't moving anymore. But around her, the enormous lions were stalking toward the finished battle. Stalking toward her mate.

"No!" she cried, pulling one of their tails hard.

It snarled and spun on her, swatted, but she was ready. She ducked out of the way.

"Beast!" she screamed in warning.

He stood slowly over his kill, eyes roiling with hatred as the five remaining council members trotted toward him. The hunters fanned out, and Beast's attention was pulled this way and that, as if deciding who to attack first. It wasn't fair.

The fight with Justin was right. It was one-on-one the way a challenge was supposed to be, but this was the council of a race of shifters putting down one of their own for no good reason.

To them, Beast was the obstacle to bringing Kiera back into line, but to her, this man was everything. And what could she do? She was stuck in her human skin.

Frantically, she searched for something to use as a weapon, but there was nothing but dirt and grass around her.

The sound of roaring was deafening, and then they were running at him. Beast didn't move to escape. His posture hummed with fury. He didn't even look surprised. Fucking council. Fucking lions.

Two of the council leapt onto him, and in the flurry of battle, the other three joined. Beast was fighting for his life, and she couldn't just stand here and watch him die. Inside of her, the lion was roaring for blood, pounding the need for violence through her veins with every pump of her heart, and before she knew what she was doing, she was sprinting for them.

She screamed as she reached them, but just as she leapt onto the pile of razor sharp claws and curved canines, something wrenched her upward by the arms. Kiera gasped. She looked up at the underbelly of a giant snowy owl. Overhead, two dragons circled, one green, one gray, and over the mountains, toward the wreck, there was a line of billowing smoke, as though one of the dragons had burned a line there. Maybe they were trying to keep the humans back.

She knew who this enormous, white feathered

owl was, flying her away from the battle, away from her love. Air Ryder Croy was here, which meant so was the Bloodrunner Crew. Below her, Logan's massive grizzly bowled into the battle, flanked by three other monstrous brown bears. Winter's panther was there, tearing into one of the lions Lucian had sent after Dustin. Dustin and Emma were brawling with the other, who was already on the defensive, slinking off between the wolves ripping his hide. Ravens circled like omens.

The crews of Kane's Mountains and Harper's Mountains had come for them.

Ryder dipped so fast her stomach dropped to the ground. He set her on the edge of the woods and circled back to the battle.

Dark Kane's terrifying dragon blotted out the sun as he stretched his black, tattered gargoyle wings and landed on the cliff above. His long, curved claws dislodged boulders, and when he roared, lava and fire spewed from his mouth.

There was utter chaos, and then the shock of complete silence. The snow was coming down so thick, Kiera couldn't see much. Tears streamed down her cheeks as she cradled her belly and searched frantically through the falling snow, her entire body trembling from shock and cold and fear. *Please, please, please let him be alive.*

A shadow appeared through the white, and a scar-faced lion limped toward her, eyes blazing, crimson dripping from him in a dozen different places. His chestnut mane was dotted with snowflakes, and his tail twitched behind him with every powerful step. He was the most beautiful sight she'd ever seen.

A sob wrenched from her throat as she bolted for him. "Beast, Beast, Beast," she chanted mindlessly.

He shifted into his human skin, but it looked painful, and he went straight down to his knees. He looked utterly exhausted, but there was a crooked smile on his lips as he covered his bleeding ribs with one arm and held out the other. He grunted when he caught her, gripped the back of her neck as she buried her face against his throat.

"I thought I lost you." She could barely get the words past her tightening vocal chords.

"I'm still here," he said in a deep, rich tone that said his lion was still at the surface. "You're safe, Kiera. You're both safe."

Safe. That word had been a dream before she'd met Beast. It had been this elusive thing she'd always wished for, but could never quite reach.

Behind his broad shoulders, the snow thinned enough to show the limp piles of the council scattered around the clearing. All of that treachery for nothing. The lions would lose their way of life or keep it. Whichever way made no difference to her. She couldn't conjure a single ounce of pity for the lions that had tried to kill her mate. For all she cared, Kane could burn them to nothing and devour all their ashes.

Ripping her gaze away from the carnage, she kissed Beast's neck, his cheeks, and then worked her way to his lips and held. They just...stayed there with their mouths pressed together as he rocked her gently. Beast eased back and rested his forehead against hers, eyes closed as he inhaled. And then he leaned into her and kissed her again, his lips softening.

When he pulled away, it was to whisper, "Tell me you're both okay."

The baby was kicking up a storm, probably thanks to the adrenaline. On her knees in the snow,

Kiera smiled emotionally and dragged his hand to her belly. The baby was putting on a good show. A bump, and Beast huffed a relieved sound and rubbed his cheek against hers in a sign of devotion. "It's over, Kitty. You don't have to run anymore."

"You're really mine?" she choked out.

"For as long as you'll have me."

Kiera lifted up and hugged his shoulders as tight as she could just to convince herself he was really still here—warm and breathing and alive and...hers. She'd found her person. She'd somehow found the man who would go to war with an entire shifter race just to keep her safe. Beast belonged to her, and she belonged to him back. This was the moment she would remember for all her life, the moment she actually got to keep her happiness. The moment she put down her first root into the future she wanted. It was the moment she got to wrap her heart around this full life with the man she loved.

The Blackwings were here now, loosely circled around them. They were clawed to hell. Kane stood beside his Roe, chin lifted high as he looked at Kiera with a knowing smile on his lips. Logan looked pale, and his chest was ripped up with fresh scars. He was recovering from Beast's attack the other night, but he was here, leaning heavily on his mate, watching Kiera and Beast with a slight grin quirking his lips. He'd gone to battle with the council for her man. So had Winter, Dustin, and Emma. So had the dragons. So had the Bloodrunners.

Home wasn't at all what she'd expected. Kiera had searched for it from the day she'd lost her mom but hadn't quite been able to pick a house. Silly her, home wasn't a house at all.

Home was a trailer park where she would raise her cub with the man she adored.

Home was the D-Team, who'd risked everything to save them today.

Home was Kane's Mountains.

She smiled emotionally at the Blackwing Crew—at *her* crew—and then she laid a kiss on the scar on her mate's face. Kiera let her lips linger on his cheek as a silent *I love you* because he had given her *everything*.

Home was Beast.

EPILOGUE

Beast blew out a steadying breath and hugged his baby boy closer in the cradle of his arm. Three days old and Beast still had trouble looking away from him. He was so *tiny*. And perfect. It was insane to think about this fragile, little boy someday growing up to be a big, brawling lion shifter.

He adjusted the blue hat and brushed his finger down the baby's round, soft cheek. In his sleep, his son made sucking motions with his mouth.

"I love when he does that," Kiera whispered from where she lay stretched out next to Beast on the couch, her head on his thigh as they watched their boy together.

"Dreaming of boobies," Beast murmured through a smile. He stroked Kiera's hair, and then pressed his finger against the baby's hand. He wrapped his small fist around Beast's finger on reflex and held it.

Kiera let off a sigh that sounded happy and slid her hand over Beast's thigh. When the content noise tapered into a growl, Beast frowned down at her. Kiera's eyes had stayed gold since she'd had the baby. Beast pulled her hand to his lips and pressed a kiss on her knuckles before he straightened the baby's hat again. He couldn't help touching them all the time now. It was like his lion was only sated if he could physically reassure himself that his little family was safe and happy.

"Are you going to call him today?" she asked.

"Are you reading my mind now?"

Her smile was beautiful as it stretched her full lips. "Maybe. Our bond has been getting stronger." She had a point. Neither one of them were fighting it, so yeah, they could damn near read each other's feelings.

And Beast was nervous for reasons he couldn't explain. Of course his intuitive mate picked up on it. She was sensitive.

He inhaled deeply and nodded. "It won't be a long call. The old silverback isn't much of a talker."

Beast eased his cell out of his back pocket and dialed one of the most important numbers he had.

"Beast." Callum greeted him in a gravelly voice that brought back a hundred lessons from childhood.

Beast pinned the phone between his ear and his shoulder so he could stroke Kiera's soft hair again. "I have news. Last week, Kiera and I officially registered to the Blackwing Crew as a mated pair. And then…" Beast shook his head as he became overwhelmed with the emotion of the words he'd never thought he would get the chance to say.

A single tear streaked out of the corner of Kiera's eye as she smiled up at him. Beautiful mate. So sweet.

Beast blew out a steadying breath and tried again after he dragged his gaze to the baby. "Three days ago Kiera gave me a boy. We named him Callum."

The old silverback chuckled warmly. Static blasted over the phone, and then in a muffled voice, he told his mate, Soren, "It's a boy. They named him after me."

Beast could make out Soren's excited laughter that almost immediately morphed into joyful crying.

More static and then Callum asked, "Are you

happy, boy?"

"Yeah, I'm happy." Beast blinked hard. "I wanted to call you sooner, but I had a lot to think about. I had a decision to make. Do you remember when you gave me the name Beast? You said that someday I wouldn't need the name anymore and I would call you and give you the name back."

There was a lengthy pause and then, "I remember. Is that time now?"

Beast traced Kiera's smiling lips with his thumb. "No. Beast is my name. It's part of my history, and the name my crew knows me by. It's the name my mate knows me by. And if someday my boy should turn into a brawler like me, and he's in need of the name Beast, perhaps I'll give it to him then, like you did for me. Until then, I'll carry it. I'll own it. I wouldn't be here without it. I wouldn't have found Kiera or this life without it."

Beast had never seen or heard the old silverback get emotional before, but Callum sniffed hard. "I'm real proud of who you became."

When his voice cracked on the last word, Beast had a hard time controlling the burning sensation in his eyes. He ran his hand down his jaw and locked gazes with Kiera. She was so damn good about giving him strength when he needed it.

Beast cleared his throat. "You taking me in like I was your own? I never thanked you for all you did for me."

"Aw, now don't get sappy on me," Callum rumbled, but now his voice was thick and breaking apart. "Tell Kiera hi and give your little mini-beast a hug from me and the missus. We'll see you in two weeks when we visit."

When the line went dead, Beast set the phone on the couch cushion beside him and shook his head in awe at how his life had ended up.

A long growl rumbled from Kiera, and she doubled in on herself like she was in pain. She'd been putting off her first Change, likely because of her maternal instincts. She was reluctant to leave little Callum even for a second.

"It's time," Beast murmured, running his fingers through her hair again. "She's been patient, Kitty. She let you keep your body all through the pregnancy. She was a good momma lioness, but you can't put her off forever."

The smile fell from Kiera's face. "What if I don't

remember how to Change?"

Beast helped her up and rocked up off the couch after her, careful not to jostle his sleeping boy. "It's okay if it doesn't go smooth the first time. You'll figure it out."

Kiera slipped her hand into his and walked out of their trailer by his side. Beast led her down the porch steps and past the fence that no longer sported the No Trespassing sign. He led her to the edge of the woods and stopped. He swayed Callum gently back and forth as Kiera meandered into a small clearing between two towering white pines.

Slowly, Kiera turned, and Beast was stunned by how stunning his mate was in the evening light. Her hair was long and curled, waving down her shoulders as she eased out of her clothes, and that sunset sure looked beautiful on her skin.

She heaved a shaky sigh. "What if it takes a long time?"

"There's no pressure. None. It's only me and Callum here watching."

"And me," Dustin called from the woods. He popped out from behind a tree like a creeper and lifted a long-lensed camera. "I've been waiting for three straight days for this. I'm taking pictures. Emma is gonna make a scrapbook. And we might do a slideshow at the next D-Team Sucks Saturday. Shift pretty, Kitty."

"Fuck off, Dustin," Beast called. "And don't call her Kitty. That's my pet name."

"I'm taking video," Winter said from farther in the woods. She stepped out with a bright smile, her round belly leading the way when she wandered closer. She would be having Kane and Rowan's baby in a few months' time. And surprise, surprise, Roe appeared behind her, making sure Winter didn't trip and fall. Her maternal instincts had kicked in so thoroughly they extended to Winter, who didn't seem to mind the devotion.

Exasperated, Beast glared at the D-Teamers. "What is happening right now? Kiera doesn't want extra eyes on her."

Logan, Kane, and Emma appeared around the corner of Beast's trailer with half-empty beer bottles in their hands. Kane handed Beast a full one.

"I'm not drinking while I'm holding a baby."

Logan's eyes narrowed in confusion. "Why not? Callum's asleep. He won't know."

"Fuckin' D-Team," Beast muttered.

"The show hasn't started yet?" Kane asked. "Come on, Kiera. Let her out already."

"I'm hungry for asparagus," Dustin said unhelpfully as he fiddled with the camera. "It makes my pee smell funny. Here, Kitty, I'll help." Dustin pulled out his cell phone and pushed a button, and the notes of a song echoed through the woods. Dustin, that dick, had recorded Beast saying, "Aw fuck, Dustin! You're my best friend!" on the phone the day Kiera had been kidnapped. And then he had paid someone to remix a song with that as the only lyrics. It was auto-tuned and everything. He'd played it about eight million times already. Beast was definitely going to choke him. Beside Beast, Emma was singing along off-key, and even Logan was tapping his foot.

Kiera's eyes went round and, slowly, she covered her full boobs, like any of the shifters here gave a single flying fart about nudity. "Uuuh, even with music, I don't think I can do this in front of everyone."

Beast looked from crew member to crew member and tried to hold an angry grimace. Wasn't working, though. A stupid smile kept trying to take over his face. It was the D-Team's fault for annoying him into smiles lately. That and this stupid song. And of course they had stalked Kiera so they could watch her first Change. He used to hate the way the crew shared everything, but that wouldn't ever change. And lately, he didn't feel like it was such an awful thing. He didn't want to let them know he was going soft, though, so shook his head in silent apology to Kiera then called out, "I hate you all."

Dustin did some sign language, and beside Beast, Emma said, "Aaaaw, he says we love you too, Beast."

"Annoying," Beast muttered, but that damn smile was back stretching his face. He sighed and handed Callum gently to Emma.

Kiera smelled scared, but she didn't need to be. He would always keep her safe. She just needed a reminder of her inner badass. Beast undressed and let his lion rip out of him. He landed on all fours and then meandered to Kiera, rubbed up against her in a tight circle. She smelled like a lioness, and he could feel her. He walked a few paces into the woods and turned. And then he lifted his head and called her animal out. He roared, over and over, softer as time went on, until Kiera's body buckled, and she fell to the forest floor. Her Change was slow and she would be sore tomorrow, but for now, she stood on all four shaky legs. And here in the muted sunset lighting, with the Blackwing Trailer Park as the backdrop behind her, Beast fell for his beautiful Kiera all over again.

Her lioness was a soft gold, her coat shining. Her body was lithe, and though her first steps were clumsy, she found her grace soon enough. It was her eyes that held him, though.

Thanks to Apex, those eyes had been frozen into her face the first time he'd met her. This animal wasn't supposed to exist anymore, but their love had brought her back. He'd waited so long to see this part of her, spent countless hours imagining what her lioness looked like, and the moment was finally here. She stood tall and proud, twitching her tail, her ears erect. She stole his breath away. He *needed* to touch her, so Beast strode up to her and rested his forehead against hers. *Hey, Kitty.* And then Beast ran his body down her length. She was much smaller than him, but she held her ground. Strong mate.

She always talked about his silent *I love yous*, and this was another one. She deserved to feel his adoration, every day, every hour. Until he drew his last breath, he would live every moment for her because she had opened his eyes and made him feel again.

When he ran his body up her other side, she was ready and rubbed her face against his.

Beast walked beside her as she strode deeper into the woods. Around them, the Blackwings gathered. In front of Beast, Logan had his arm thrown over Winter's shoulders as she chattered on about how good Kiera had done for her first Change. Rowan followed closely behind Winter, swatting at a bug that almost landed on her. Dark Kane chuckled warmly at his mate and pulled her in close before he kissed the top of her head. Behind Beast, Dustin clicked away on his camera as that damn best friend song played on and on. Beside the wolf walked Emma. A soft smile curved her lips as she looked down at little Callum cradled in her arms. She cooed the song to him. That little cub was going to grow up completely adored by this crew of dysfunctional maniacs. Beast and Kiera had somehow found their cub a pride, only so much better.

The D-Team was a chaotic, incessantly

obnoxious, perfect mess.

They were *his* mess.

Beast had thought he never wanted to be close to anyone again, but look what had happened? This crew of crazies had somehow pried his hardened heart open. Kiera had come in and filled all the holes, and then his baby boy had broken the rest of his walls down completely. Feeling didn't hurt anymore.

Kiera sometimes spoke of how he'd saved her, but she didn't see. She was the one who had saved him. Beast had thought he was destined for an empty existence, but she'd given him a life that was better than anything he could've dreamed. His stone heart had been shattered, but had been pieced back together by the woman who had refused to give up on him, and because of her, he now believed in magic.

He believed in love, and his crew.

He believed in fate, and hope, and 10:10 wishes.

He believed in his brave Kiera, the family they were building, and the future that stretched out in front of them.

And for the rest of always, Beast would be the protector of what he'd found here in Kane's Mountains.

Want more of these characters?

Blackwing Beast is the third book in a three book series based in Kane's Mountains.

Check out these other books from T. S. Joyce.

Blackwing Defender
(Kane's Mountains, Book 1)

Blackwing Wolf
(Kane's Mountains, Book 2)

Also, if you would like to read Kane and Rowan's story, it can be found in the final book of the Harper's Mountains series.

Blackwing Dragon
(Harper's Mountains, Book 5)

About the Author

T.S. Joyce is devoted to bringing hot shifter romances to readers. Hungry alpha males are her calling card, and the wilder the men, the more she'll make them pour their hearts out. She werebear swears there'll be no swooning heroines in her books. It takes tough-as-nails women to handle her shifters.

Experienced at handling an alpha male of her own, she lives in a tiny town, outside of a tiny city, and devotes her life to writing big stories. Foodie, wolf whisperer, ninja, thief of tiny bottles of awesome smelling hotel shampoo, nap connoisseur, movie fanatic, and zombie slayer, and most of this bio is true.

Bear Shifters? Check

Smoldering Alpha Hotness? Double Check

Sexy Scenes? Fasten up your girdles, ladies and gents, it's gonna to be a wild ride.

> For more information on T. S. Joyce's work,
> visit her website at
> www.tsjoyce.com

Printed in Great Britain
by Amazon